The people and events portrayed in this novel are fictional.
Any resemblance to actual persons, living or otherwise,
is unintentional.

Hollow Bridge Publishing

Unthinkable Sins
A NOVEL

Tiffani Quarles-Sanders

UNTHINKABLE SINS
Copyright © 2015 by Tiffani Quarles-Sanders
Editor: Wendy Robinson

❧ PROLOGUE ❧

This is a crazy world we live in. It don't make no sense to me at all, how people want to think that if somebody gets hurt or wronged, or has anything taken away from them, that they won't turn around and do the same thing to somebody else. And when you do, it don't mean you not a good, God-fearing person; it just means experience has taught you well. Still, with everything I've been through, I never stopped going to church on Sunday, never stopped tithing when I could, never stopped praying to the Lord to have mercy on the souls of the dead who know the things I've done. Did I covet? Did I kill? Did I lie or plan to steal? The people who know me would find it unthinkable for my soul to be stained with such sin, but I know one thing. Suffering don't make you a saint and neither does sacrifice.

All I ever wanted was just to be loved.

- Hattie Durham

"**G**et your damn hands off me!" screamed the elderly, dark-skinned woman wearing her signature salt-and-pepper, tightly-curled wig, looking confused but filled with fight and anger. She continued to scream at the two nurses who were trying to restrain her in a small hospital bed. There was another female standing at the foot of the bed, writing information on several forms.

In the back near the exit door stood a tall man whose facial structure closely resembled that of the old woman. He contained his distress at her behavior, forcing himself to allow the hospital staff to do their jobs. They dealt with this sort of thing all the time.

"Didn't I tell you all to get your damn hands off of me," the old lady continued to rail at the staff. The woman with the forms moved closer and said "Mrs. Durham, Mrs. Durham, please calm down. We are going to help you. Now, how are you today?"

The staffer's sweet voice failed to placate the agitated old woman.

"What do you mean, 'how am I today?' Right now, I'm doing bad, bad, because y'all trying to kill me!" she said.

"No, ma'am. We are going to do all we can to

help you feel better," the staffer replied.

"You can't do a damn thing for me, woman. I know what you are trying to do," the old woman said menacingly. "You are just trying to take my money. Let me tell you, you ain't taking my money. I will kill you first. You hear me. I will kill all of you."

"Ma'Dear, stop acting like that. These people are trying to help you," the man standing by the door said. He entered the room as if he had been dreading the moment and approached his mother, who had finally been restrained on the bed. Jerome Durham sighed. He hated seeing her like this.

This woman he had known all of his life had grown increasingly ornery over the past few months, but he had never seen her this angry before. She seemed almost vicious. Yes, he thought wearily, it's time. Time to do something about her. The thought gave him no peace.

Hattie twisted and turned from side to side as though she truly thought to escape the hand restraints that tied her to the sides of her bed. Meanwhile, the woman with the forms shifted her attention to the man. "Are you her son?"

"Yes, ma'am, I am. Jerome. Jerome Durham," he said. He leaned forward to shake the young woman's hand. Her eyes widened briefly with recognition.

"Oh, yes, of course. Councilman Durham," she said. "I'm Dr. Olivia Thomas, and I'm the primary physician at this facility."

"Pleased to meet you. Please excuse my mother. She's a little upset," Jerome apologized.

"It's to be expected. This is all new to her," the doctor said reassuringly. "We'll have you settled in here in no time, won't we, Mrs. Durham?"

She leaned over and patted Hattie's hand. Sedated now, Hattie pushed the doctor's hand off her own. She shrugged and settled back into the pillows, still muttering angrily.

"I've gone over your mother's medical history, and I know her condition has been deteriorating for awhile. But how long has she been like this?"

Eager for the chance to drown out his mother's embarrassing chatter, Jerome explained to the doctor that small signs had been showing for more than a month. There had been an incident in which she'd accused her granddaughter of stealing her purse. "We found the purse under the bed," he recalled. "Then she called me and said that someone stole her clothes. When I got to her house and checked her room, all her clothes was gone," he went on. "I noticed that her dog was not in the house, so I went to look for him outside. Her clothes were piled up in the backyard and burnt to a crisp." Jerome shook his head at the still-puzzling memory.

"My goodness," Dr. Thomas responded.

"We just thank God she wasn't hurt," Jerome said. "After that, we knew we couldn't leave her by herself anymore, so my brothers and I, along with our kids, all take turns staying with her. We could not get her to move in with us," he added. Hattie glared at him.

"Jerome, why in the world you telling this woman my business? And your ass is lying on me anyway. I wouldn't do such a thing to my own clothes. I am a Christian woman." Hattie was indignant. She went to fold her arms, but restraints held her wrists firmly at her sides. She started to struggle again.

"Now, Ma'Dear," Jerome began to soothe her, but Hattie wasn't having it. She tried to sit straight up to show how mad she was, but she was starting to feel so sleepy. She fell to muttering again.

"Well, Mr. Durham, as we get in results, I may be asking more questions from time to time," Dr. Thomas commanded his attention again. "We will keep her here over night for testing and observation. However, we would like to send her over to our other unit that specializes in geriatric mental care. She will be seen by our specialist as well as a psychiatrist. "

"That's fine," Jerome responded. "I know my family will not have a problem with having her observed - we just want her to get better. But once she realizes that she has to stay, she is going to have a fit." He closed his eyes and placed his forehead in his hand. The doctor gave him a moment to compose himself.

"All of this administrative stuff will be over soon," Dr. Thomas said. "Someone will come around to verify her insurance information and have you sign some release forms. As soon as we get back her test results, I will contact you and your family to go over your mother's needs."

As Jerome looked with concern over his mother's prone form, the doctor touched his elbow.

"Councilman Durham," she said. "Please get some rest tonight. Your mother is in excellent hands and you did the right thing by bringing her here. We can address the issues now, and everyone can feel more secure."

"Thank you so much, "Jerome said. He watched distractedly as the doctor proceeded down the hall, stopping at the nurse's station to review her notes.

As he reached for the door to her room, Jerome was suddenly overwhelmed with emotion. He had to tell his mother that she would not be going home tonight. That news might destroy her calm, even if she was on medication. The upsetting truth was that his mother might not ever be going home again. Opening the door, Jerome slowly walked into the room.

"Where the hell you been, Jerome?" Hattie said angrily. "You know today is Sunday, and I got to get to church on time. I can't find my purse. Where's my damn purse? " As she tried to lift her hands, she realized once again that they were tied down to her bed.

"Lord, Jerome, those bad-ass kids of yours have tied me down with all this mess. I wish you and that wife of yours would go ahead and whip them like you know how. I would have stopped this a long time ago," she went on. "They going to be whipping y'all when they get grown. That oldest one, Junior, ain't no older than nine years old, and he's already jail material thanks to you." Hattie continued to mutter, only partially aware of her conversation with him it seemed. As he listened to her, Jerome was becoming more and more convinced that staying at the facility was the best choice for his mother.

Her statements were becoming more and more mixed up. She clearly had no concept of time and seemed to float in and out of it, mixing present with past, then back to the present again. Jerome didn't know what bothered him more : the fact that today was not Sunday but Monday, and she had attended church with her family just the day before, or the fact that she referred to his children as kids when they were now grown with their own families. His oldest son Junior was no boy of nine, but had just turned 29 years old this year.

However, the statements his mother made about how he and his wife raised their children really cut Jerome to the core. It made him think. Is this what she thought all this time while he was raising his kids? Did she ever tell her feelings to others behind his back? Is she saying all of this now because she cannot control herself?

A scary thought came to his mind. If his mother really could not control herself and started speaking out on just anything and everything, who knew what she might say? One thing for sure, if she continued to talk out like this and he did not get her under control, she was going to embarrass not only him but the whole family. What if her neighbors or worse, the church members, came by to visit and she is this belligerent and talking with such a filthy mouth?

Jerome was horrified by the thought. Everyone who knew Hattie Durham respected her as a good and faithful member of Shiloh Missionary Baptist Church, where she had served as Missionary President for 30 years.

What if she can't stop talking, and she starts telling all the family secrets to anyone who would listen? Jerome's thoughts were racing. He was actually sweating. Maybe, he thought, we should just tell people that right now she can't have visitors yet. But knowing the folks in that church, they are going to be doing a lot of talking. One thing I know for sure is we need to get her under control, he thought. There was too much at stake if they didn't. He was in the middle of running for a higher office.

Jerome pulled a handkerchief from his front shirt pocket and wiped his forehead. Once again, he stepped closer to his mother's bed.

"Ma'Dear," he spoke comfortingly to her. "You know you took good care of us when we was little."

Hattie slowly sat up in her bed and said, "Yeah, that was my job."

"Well, mother, now it is time for us to look after you. I have these good people here that are going to take good care of you and make sure that you have everything you need. I'll be back in the morning to check on you." Jerome leaned over to kiss her cheek, but Hattie raised her hand to stop him.

"Wait a minute," she said, looking around. "This look like a hospital. I know you aren't going to leave me at no hospital." Jerome sighed.

"Yes, ma'am, this is a hospital. You need to be here to get medicine and stuff we don't have for you at home," he explained. But Hattie was not having it.

"Lord, you know one thing I did not ever do to you was leave you somewhere and not take you home. When I took you to the doctor, I always brought you back home," she moaned. "I never, ever, left you like you are doing me. You ought to be ashamed of yourself."

Hiding his dismay, Jerome squared his shoulders. Standing in the background, the nurse saw how Hattie's comments affected her handsome son.

She spoke kindly to him. "Mr. Durham, the medicine we gave her earlier will help her sleep. Why don't you go on home now, and she will rest."

Indeed, Hattie was finding it harder and harder to keep her eyes open. A few seconds later, she started to snore softly. Jerome gave a sigh of relief. He patted his mother hand with real tenderness.

"Mr. Durham, my name is Lisa," the nurse said. "I will

be looking after your mother while she's here."

"Thank you," Jerome said. "I know she's in good hands here."

"I know that it's hard on you to see her like this, but, believe me, you're doing the best thing for her," Lisa said.

"Trust me. I have seen many cases like this before. The names of the patients are different but many of the cases are the same. They always seem to lash out at the ones that are closest to them," she said, leaning over and pulling Hattie's covers up. She turned back to him. "When that happens, you must remember that this is not how your mother really feels. It is just the sickness talking."

Jerome found her smile reassuring.

"I am going to leave now, but I will be back in the morning," he said. "If you need to contact me, please do.

"Lisa's heart swelled with compassion as she watched Jerome's retreating form. That poor man, she thought. His mother said some mean things to him. But time can heal this. Miss Hattie will feel better in the morning, and it's likely she won't remember her cruel words to her son.

Lisa checked her patient one last time, then left the room. As the lights went out, Hattie murmured softly in her sleep. Her mind was struggling through layers of some kind of thick fog. It was so hard to see anything and even harder to think. It was a scary place for a little girl. A place she remembered. They had left her all alone here. And it was all her fault.

CHAPTER TWO

That morning had been a busy one as Hattie's whole family got up early and took off for the three-hour walk down the road to Ella's sister Marlene's place. It was a long walk and a rare leisurely time for the family together. The children played along the way and sometimes ran ahead.

Their arrival had seemed celebratory as well. It was always good to see other family again. Marlene and her husband, Roby, had two daughters just a little younger than Hattie. The children ran off to play. Everything had been fine until Hattie's sister, Viola, started gathering the other children around her. Viola said she had something to tell. Hattie saw the serious look on Viola's face.

"Hattie's not going with us when we leave to home today," the older girl said. She looked at her little sister. "That's why Mama made you bring your clothes with you."

"No, sir!" Hattie retorted. But she was worried. When Mama wrapped up the few clothes she owned and handed them to her wrapped in a rag, Hattie had wondered why she was the only one bringing her belongings, but she had not dared to ask. Running and playing with the other kids all morning had made her forget. Now she scowled at Viola.

"It's true!" Viola stated. Hattie started to cry.

"Why they gone leave me?" she wailed.

"Daddy say it cause Hoot's so dark and ugly!" Her brother, James, pitched in. There was an uncomfortable silence as the other children stared at Hattie. No one disputed the cruel remark. The children were used to hearing their father say things like that. Viola felt sorry for Hattie and put her arm around her baby sister.

"That ain't true," she said. "Mama was talking to Daddy, and he said it would be better for you 'til you big enough to work and earn your keep. Ain't enough food in the house for him to feed someone who can't do nothing to help the family."

"If it wasn't for Hattie's big mouth we wouldn't have to worry," James said. The boy was venting his own anxiety by directing his anger at Hattie.

"No, sir," Hattie protested again. But in her heart she was afraid he was right. Hattie feared everything James had said was true.

First of all, she had known all of her life that her father did not think she was attractive. He thought she was just a useless, ugly girl, neither worthy of much attention nor the effort it took to raise her. When she was born, Benton had sat there drinking, not interested in seeing or holding the new baby. His wife and her sister, who had come to help with the birth, thought it was because he had been hoping for a boy. Lord knew that was what everyone else was hoping for.

But if Benton Halsey knew people thought he was disappointed at the baby's sex, he would have just shrugged. First of all, he didn't take it as any offense or slur on his manhood; a man did it to his woman with the same strength it took to get a girl as it did a boy. It was no different. Had Benton been measuring the virtues of having a son over a daughter he might have had come to some surprising conclusions. While a son could lend his shoulders to the labor of life, he could also grow up to rival the rooster for the available hens. Benton had heard of that happening. A daughter would be a cook and a maid and a mother and countless other things. Benton had heard tell of that too. But a boy or a girl was all the same to him: just another mouth to feed.

His wife, apologetic for the disappointment she also thought he felt over fathering a daughter, had suggested that they name the baby Hattie, after his mother. After a moment, he agreed. His mother would have been pleased to know that her name at least continued to be heard in the world. But as baby Hattie added months to her young life, it seemed like the name was all she would ever have in common with his mother besides blood, and even that was seriously in question. His mother had been a nice-looking woman: sweet-mouthed and brown-skinned with a healthy build. Her namesake had not inherited those qualities.

Benton was not a man given to making much over anybody's baby. He thought most of them looked alike and were generally unremarkable. In Benton's experience, though, most improved in looks over time. That didn't seem to be the case with this little girl. Little Hattie's lower lip stuck out, as if she had been struck and permanently maimed. She had a strong blocky nose that resembled no other that any one on either side of the family could remember, a fact which created a convenient, sneaking suspicion against the virtue of the girl's mother. It gave folks a reason to disclaim the innocent, dark-skinned child as a relative.

Benton could not decide whether Hattie Eloise's dark color reminded him more of creek bottom mud or cold ashes. Maybe bottom mud with cold ashes mixed in. That was it. The man's humor at his baby daughter's expense made him slap his thigh and laugh. He lit another cigarette and stared at her kicking in the cradle.

"Hattie, huh," he said. "All right, then, Hattie. But you don't look like my mother at all. You look like my foot." Those were the first words Hattie Eloise Broadnax heard from her father in her young life: his telling her she resembled his field-worn, chafed, and ugly appendage. Benton meanly warmed to his theme. "Your real name can be Hattie, but I'm gonna call you Hoot, 'cause you just like a foot. The 'H' is for Hattie, the rest is for foot."

The father's resentment at his circumstances made him childish and spiteful at the expense of his innocent new daughter. Benton didn't really mean anything by it, but the ugly nickname he gave Hattie stuck. Being called "Hoot" by everyone was a constant reminder of her father's low opinion of her looks.

If someone thought you were ugly, that was a matter of opinion and that certainly wasn't Hattie's fault. It was the other part of her brother James' accusations that hurt Hattie the most, because now the whole family was going hungry because of her mouth, because of something she had said.

Benton's brother, Winston, had come to visit. Winston had a good paying job up in Chicago and was generally considered to be way better off than Benton his sharecropping brother . The brothers had a good natured relationship, and Benton felt genuine pleasure at seeing his brother's good fortune.

Benton needed to go into town, so Winston gave him a ride. He had driven a fairly clean buckboard with two good horses all this way to see his brother, and he was happy to do it. Hattie and her brother George were home that day and got to ride along. The excited children climbed up on the buckboard. Along the way, the brothers talked, Benton confiding in Winston some of the hardships he was facing, not the least of which was the fact that he was trying to provide for Ella and their five kids together, but also his other woman, who had just given birth. Winston sighed at his brother's behavior. Despite all of his hardships, Benton still found time to chase skirts.

As his brother talked, Winston leaned back to whisper to Hattie, giving her two pennies to buy some candy for herself and her brother. Hattie's eyes went round as she stared at the money in her hand. She thanked her uncle and then turned back to show her brother. They spent the rest of the ride trading boasts about their generous uncle.

"He's rich," Hattie said in wonder.

"He rich, that make us rich, too," George declared.

Once they got to town, Winston let George help him tie up the horses. The children were sent to the general store with orders to come right back outside and wait by the buckboard while the two grownups did business across the street.

Hattie felt important as the balding white man at the counter leaned over to take her money.

"That's a lot of candy you got there," he said. "Y'all sure you got enough money to pay for it?" Hattie nodded, proudly showing her two pennies. The man's smile turned mean.

"How come you got all this money to buy so much candy, little girl?"

Hattie was still buoyant from the ride. "'Cause we rich!" she stated triumphantly. She knew it was the wrong thing to say the moment the words left her lips. The white man's smile now turned menacing. He could not have his ragged, poor, and black tenant's daughter waving money around his store and bragging about it. Hattie heard George gasp.

"I mean, my uncle's rich," she amended, barely whispering. It was too late. The man slapped the counter and took her money.

"That's good," he said. "That means he'll be able to help your poor daddy pay me what he still owes me."

"You tell your daddy I'm coming out there, and he better have my money, since you all so rich," the man sneered. He turned to take the next person in line. George grabbed Hattie by the arm, and they ran out of the store, not saying anything until they had started along the road home. Halfway there, they noticed dust rising on the road a mile or so behind them. Someone was in furious pursuit.

"Hattie told Mr. Lamar we was rich," George yelled quickly.

The next minutes were spent in a tense dash for the house with a group on horseback close on their tail. George was sent to cut across the land to warn Ella but the little time it bought was worthless against Mr. Lamar's false claims against their family. He said Benton still owed $40 against the crop.

When Benton told him that he didn't have the money, Mr. Lamar laughed.

"Then just borrow it from your rich brother," he spat.

The posse of men with him went out and stripped the buckboard of the supplies Winston and Benton had bought. All they could do was stand and watch as the men went through the home and garden, knocking over the family's few possessions and removing the food they had stored for the winter. Ella, Hattie, and George clung to one another, crying.

"Mr. Lamar, please," Ella begged. Benton warned her to be quiet.

The landlord gestured to his men. They teamed up on Winston and Benton, restraining them while Mr. Lamar removed the bills from each man's wallet. Winston's eyes were disbelieving. Not only had he bought things to supply both his brother's households, he had also given Bennett a little spending cash. Now it was all gone, including his own money.

"I'll take this into account with this other stuff we got here, and I'll let you know what you still owe, Benton," Mr. Lamar said. Benton glared at him, knowing he had no way to prove that the landlord had falsified his account of what was truly owed on the crop share. He knew Jedediah Lamar was really sending a personal message to stay away from Bessie Holmes, a nice-looking woman who had moved in down the road. It wasn't fair of the man to take it out on the family like this, but Benton had no recourse. He hung his head.

Mr. Lamar looked around and smiled.

"I guess that about does it," he said. In a last gesture of meanness, he singled out little Hattie and said,

"Your sorry uncle don't look so rich no more. Hope y'all like that candy."

The household was in shock. There was little anyone could say. The children were frightened silent. Of the adults, no one wanted to relive the humiliation they had just gone through by talking about it. Embarrassed, Winston just wanted to get back to Chicago. There, he could feel like a man again. He felt sorry for his brother.

Benton sat down with a sigh. His wife stood by and put her hands on his shoulders, but he shook her off angrily. He was too upset to be comforted.

For a moment, Hattie stood there taking it all in. She was learning that the South was a mean place for people of color in those times. It was a place where a man could rob another man's family and get away with it just because he was white. It was a place where a man could beat his wife and children just because he was a man.

Men weren't the only ones who committed those kinds of sins either. A woman like Bessie Holmes could have all kinds of men, black or white, married or not, running through her house and still take charity from women like Hattie's mother, who hated to see little children go hungry. Hattie remembered plenty of times that her mother had sent food up to the Holmes' place, knowing that Bessie had no way to earn a living other than what she got for her favors from different men. People could hurt you, lie to you, and steal from you, and get away with it. Yes, Hattie Eloise Halsey was learning a lot from the things going on around her. Benton suddenly slammed a hand down on the table, making his wife jump.

Hattie hurriedly avoided her father and ran outside after her brothers who had gone on a hasty hunt for the family's supper that night. What had happened was awful. And it was her fault.

And now Viola and James, George and Annie, too, and even Mama would be sent out to work extra jobs to pay what Lamar said Benton owed. They would be lucky to scrape together their daily meals. It would be a hard winter for Hattie's family. If anybody thought it would be easier for her living with her aunt and her husband and two kids, they were wrong. But Hattie didn't have any say in it.

When they left her there, Hattie ran after them, crying. Her Aunt Marlene went after her, picked her up, and brought her back. She laid the child down on a pallet and sat there with her for a minute before leaving the room. Her two daughters, Doe and Pudge, entered the room. After a while, the two curious girls came over to comfort their cousin, but little Hattie wasn't even aware of their presence as she sobbed herself to sleep. Her family had left her behind.

❦ CHAPTER THREE ❧

Waking up meant swimming through layers of confusion for Hattie. Spending the night in a strange place had been hard. The last thing she remembered was Mama and them leaving her behind despite her pleas to go home with them. But they had left her anyway.

Wait, no, that had been a long time ago. Hattie shook her head. She had been dreaming about her childhood. She was a grown woman now with grown children of her own. Last night her son Jerome had been the last familiar face Hattie remembered seeing. Still, her surroundings now were unfamiliar.

"Good afternoon, Mrs. Durham. I'm Lisa. I will be your nurse again tonight." The older woman opened her eyes slowly, trying to connect a face to the voice. As her eyes focused on the source, she lifted her head and smiled a great smile.

"Oh, yes, baby. Say your name again?"

Lisa spoke a little louder. "Lisa, ma'am. My name is Lisa."

"I'm glad to meet you, Lisa. I am Mrs. Durham, Mrs. Hattie Durham. Did you say you were my nurse last night?" Hattie's expression wrinkled with confusion. "I'm sure I was at home last night."

"No, ma'am, you were here, and I took good care of you. The same way I'm going to do tonight, don't you worry," Lisa said. She busied herself tidying Hattie's linen.

"Thank you, Baby, for taking good care of me because, Lord knows, them kids and grandkids sure ain't," Hattie replied. She shook herself grouchily.

"Ma'am, I'm sure your family loves you," Lisa responded. "Let's get you like some ice water, Mrs. Durham. You need to stay hydrated." Lisa poured from a stainless steel pitcher on the table by Hattie's bed. Inside, Hattie was smiling with pleasure. It was sure nice to have someone waiting on her this way.

"Tell me something more about your family, Mrs. Durham," Lisa said. "How many children do you have?"

"Oh, I have three boys," Hattie chuckled to herself as she sipped her water.

"Oh, yes. I remember that one of your sons was here last night," Lisa said. She saw the look of confusion on Mrs. Durham's face. "He said he was your youngest," she added to help the old woman out.

"Oh, yes, that must have been my Jerome," Hattie said. "He's a councilman with the city government, you know," she couldn't help adding proudly. She closed her eyes and sipped again from her glass. When she looked up again, she looked strangely at the nurse as if she were seeing her for the first time.

"Baby, what's your name again?"

The young woman smiled patiently. "Lisa," she responded.

"Oh, yes, Lisa. That's a pretty name," the old woman smiled again. "You got kids, too?"

"Yes, ma'am, two of them. I have a little boy, André Jr. — we call him AJ — and my youngest, Kayla.

They are ten and eight years old."

"Oh, I bet they are just beautiful," Hattie exclaimed. She understood the pride in the young woman's voice as she talked about her family. Her own three sons, Lewis, Jr., Carl, and Jerome had been the source of much joy, as well as some trouble and heartache, too. Too much trouble and heartache, Hattie thought.

She leaned closer to Lisa. "You married or do you just 'got a man,' like these young women say nowadays?"

"Yes, ma'am, I'm married. My husband's name is name is André Garvin, Sr."

"How long y'all been married, Baby?"

Lisa spoke carefully. Sometimes old people had old-fashioned ideas. She didn't want to offend her patient, but she had to be truthful.

"We been together close to fifteen years, but married for just eight," she said. "Mrs. Durham, I need to lift you up in your bed a little and fix your pillows."

Hattie allowed the younger woman to reposition her. She settled back onto the pillows with a sneaky grin and said, "So you had the baby first, then y'all got married after, huh?"

Lisa paused a moment before answering. She hadn't meant for things to get so personal, but she was a truthful girl. "Yes, ma'am," she said simply. Hattie clucked.

"Lord have mercy on y'all young folks. You girls just have babies from this man and that," she fussed. Then the grin returned.

"Well, I guess you did okay since Old Tom married you. I went to your wedding, remember? I was there," Hattie continued. "Your mama, Mattie, and your daddy, Harry, was there too. How is your old daddy doing?"

Lisa quickly realized that Hattie's dementia was obviously influencing the conversation. She knew nothing of this older woman, having just met her yesterday. Her parents were not named Mattie and Harry, and Mrs. Durham surely had not attended her wedding at the courthouse.

Lisa thought it best to just let Hattie talk. She had family members of her own who suffered from this dreadful disease, and she had seen many patients in this state as well. It could be therapeutic for folks to go ahead and talk themselves through whatever little part of the past they were reliving. Eventually, the old woman would work herself back around to the present. Keeping her calm was the important thing.

Lisa tuned in to hear the conversation Mrs. Durham was now having with herself. "Yes, yes, Baby, I loved going to your Grandmamma Lucy's house in the country when I was a little girl. She used to let us pick them sweet berries in her back yard. And when we finished, ooo-whee, she made the best tea cakes in Lowndes and us little girls would eat, eat, eat."

Lisa smiled and responded, "Yes, ma'am."

Hattie chuckled. "Your Grandmamma Lucy sure was a good woman. She always treated us children so good. You know, every child is a blessing, and you should treat them good no matter how they come to this world."

"Yes, ma'am," Lisa agreed.

There was a knock on the door followed by a familiar male voice saying, "Hello, Ma'Dear. Can we come in?"

Hattie's handsome son, Jerome, strode into the room. He cut an imposing figure in his perfectly tailored suit. A light-skinned woman with a highly-styled coiffure followed close behind him. Hattie's smile at seeing her son faded visibly at the sight of the woman.

"How are you this evening, Mother?" Jerome asked. "Hello again, Lisa. I believe she's looking a bit better, don't you? She certainly seems calmer." He turned around to talk with the nurse, leaving Hattie and his companion looking at one another with obvious dislike. The young woman spoke first.

"How are you, Mother Durham?"

Jerome saved Hattie from having to respond. "Oh, yes, and Lisa, this is my wife, Susan Durham."

The two young women greeted each other as Hattie leaned back against her pillows with a sigh. Jerome turned back toward her. She sat up again and peered at him closely.

"Is that you, Raymond?"

Jerome looked behind him to see if someone else had entered the room. Only the nurse and his wife were there. Susan reached for his hand as Lisa went to Hattie's side and began her routine checks. Jerome leaned close to Hattie.

"Mama, it's Jerome."

His voice was calm, but Jerome was starting to worry. It wasn't the first time his mother had called him "Raymond," whoever that was. It seemed to be someone she had known in the past, and that's what worried her son now. Increasingly, Hattie's mind would dart away to sometime and someplace in her past and she would start talking. Who knew what she might say – and to whom? Jerome met his wife's eyes and knew she was thinking the same thing. They had to keep Hattie under control.

℘ CHAPTER FOUR ℘

In the following days, Jerome watched his mother growing physically stronger under the hospital's expert care. The nurses were all competent and efficient, administering to her with tenderness and respect despite her frequent memory lapses and angry outbursts. Hattie thrived under their attention. She especially seemed fond of Lisa, the attractive night nurse who went out of her way to keep her patient calm and entertained. Although his mother's physical health was stabilizing, her mental state continued to be a problem. The dementia that had claimed her mind would only continue to get worse.

Even before receiving the recommendation from Hattie's doctors, Jerome had started making plans for Hattie to be placed into long-term care. He loved his mother but he was a busy man with ongoing political business to consider. She needed medication and constant supervision, and it was simply getting to be too much to handle her at home. He certainly couldn't ask his wife to take on any more responsibility for the cantankerous old woman. Susan was as much a part of his campaign as he was, and he needed her rested and beautiful for the appearances they constantly had to make as an up-and-coming young black couple in the political spotlight. Neither of them had the time nor the expertise to properly care for Hattie at home.

Not that his wife would have, anyway. She and Hattie had never gotten along well, although, to be honest, it was not for lack of trying on Susan's part. She had been unfailingly polite, if somewhat remote, to "Ma'Dear" from the first time he'd introduced them. But for all of her impeccable debutante manners, Susan had somehow failed to win his mother over. It wasn't just that Hattie distrusted Susan, she had always just seemed to dislike her. Even before all the trouble they'd been through, Hattie seemed to have something against the young woman who had her son so smitten. Her mouth had turned down at the first glimpse of Susan Chalfont's hazel gray eyes and copper-gold curls. Jerome knew Susan reminded Hattie of someone she'd once known and maybe even hated, but that wasn't Susan's fault, was it?

Hattie had made her feelings known early on that she did not approve of that "boogie" girl her son had chosen, but Jerome had put his foot down. He thought Susan Chalfont was the most beautiful woman he had ever seen, and he couldn't believe his own luck in winning her over. Hattie would just have to deal with it.

Jerome knew that, of her three sons, he had always been his mother's favorite. Everybody knew it, though no one could have said for certain why. For the first time in his life, he traded in on it. He knew Hattie would do anything to make sure that her Jerome got what he wanted, and he wanted Susan. So Hattie had done her part and promised not to stand in the way. Susan had agreed to marry Jerome, and she and Hattie had held an uneasy truce all these years in the interest of the son and the husband they both loved.

The truce was beginning to crumble these last few months, though, along with Ma'Dear's deteriorating mind. Hattie no longer seemed interested in holding her tongue and spoke exactly what was on her mind nowadays, often insulting and berating his wife. Jerome often found himself caught in the middle. Susan was getting tired of it and was after him to do something about his mother before she caused serious damage to his campaign. Not only did she need to be someplace where she could receive the necessary medical attention, there needed to be some way to keep her from dredging up past events that would have people asking questions.

Hattie perused her daughter-in-law. She might as well have been a white woman, with that light skin and hair, and those blue eyes. Susan's pale features reminded her of someone else. A lady she had known a long time ago by the name of Helen Jane.

Hattie sat up as the night nurse paused in the doorway, calling out politely as she entered the room.

"Doe!" Hattie cried out. "Doe, is that you? After all these years." She beamed as Lisa came closer.

"Now, Miss Hattie," Lisa said. "Remember me, Lisa? How are you doing tonight?"

Hattie patted the young woman's hands and continued to chatter.

"It's so good to see you after all this time, Doe. Girl, I want to thank you for all of your letters and prayers, and for keeping in touch over the years," Hattie said. Lisa smiled and set to work around Hattie as the old woman talked. She was clearly deep in her memories, and it kept her calm while Lisa got her work done. There was no reason to disturb Mrs. Durham's reverie.

"You always were my best friend," Hattie continued. When she had gone to live with her Aunt Marlene, her cousins Dorothea and Pudge had become like her new sisters to her. Doe was a brown-skinned girl and people made a lot of her beauty. Her nickname, Doe, was both short for Dorothea and a reference to her finely shaped eyes.

Her younger sister, Patricia, called Pudge, was a butterball with long, shiny thick braids. Everyone was enamored with the girl's long hair, and so excused her for being too fat and a little slow. She was a cheerful and loyal girl, and she and her sister, Doe, made Hattie feel at home in their mother's house.

Being left behind by her family had been hard, but Marlene's family had welcomed Hattie and made her one of their own. Aunt Marlene made her living as a seamstress. She taught Hattie, who quickly surpassed her cousins in her skill with a needle and thread, though Doe was good at the weaver's art. Not too many people still made the decorative mats and hats at which she excelled.

"Girl, I never did say thank you for what you did for me that summer that Aunt Helen came," said Hattie somberly, remembering a tearful day long ago in her past. A day that would have been much worse if it hadn't been for her sweet cousin, Doe.

Helen Jane was an adult cousin of their mothers. She was a beautician, having recently attended classes to become one of Madame CJ Walkers' hair culturists. She had written ahead that she was coming to visit, stopping first to see Mama and them, and then traveling on to see Marlene and her family. Hattie, Doe, and Pudge had gone down to the depot to meet her.

Helen Jane was an elegant woman so pale and well-dressed that the little girls would never have suspected she was their relative if she had not approached them first. Among her luggage was a beautiful leather bag that held her beautician's tools, including hot irons and oils for straightening and styling hair.

Helen Jane's shiny dark hair was easily straightened with little more than a hard brush and some water. It was a great advertisement to entice other women to pay to have their hair straightened. The family had recently invested in the schooling and tools for Helen to earn her living doing just that, but she had already gone through all the women that lived in her immediate community. In order to make decent money, she had to branch out, hence, the reason for her visit.

She could make more money and gain additional clients as a traveling beautician, bringing her services to women who lived in the outlying towns and enclaves. Helen thought to get her enterprise started by visiting with immediate relatives, doing their hair for free, then appearing with them at church gatherings and the like where other women would pay for her services.

Aunt Marlene went first and Hattie thought she looked like a movie star must look. She kept exclaiming and patting her hair, made shiny and smooth by Aunt Helen's hot irons. Next came Doe. Aunt Helen took special care with the little girl, insisting that her looks would someday win beauty contests. Delighted with the results, Doe kept shaking her freshly curled pony tails, making them bounce and swing against her face.

Then it was Hattie's turn. Nervous and anxious,

she climbed into the big wooden chair in the middle of the kitchen. She watched Doe swinging her curls. She couldn't wait to do that, too. But no one could have known Hattie would be allergic to the thick, perfumed dressing oil that Aunt Helen used to straighten hair. Her scalp began to itch as soon as the substance touched her skin. Hattie began to squirm.

"Sit still, now, girl," Aunt Helen said. Hattie was determined to be good. How she wanted to have straight shiny hair like Doe's. She tried to sit still but the itchy feeling was now crawling down her skin and neck, and soon consumed her entire skin.

"Sit still!" Aunt Helen commanded. Hattie heard a hiss and smelled smoke as Aunt Helen applied the hot iron to the tuft of hair she held in her hand. The sensation of heat so close to her already uncomfortable skin made Hattie jump. She cried out as the burning comb made contact with her scalp. Startled, Aunt Helen dropped the comb. She started to reprimand the girl, who was now howling in pain.

"Hattie," Aunt Helen started to say, but she was now looking at the girl's scalp in horror. Angry red bumps were rising along the rows where she had applied the oil. A dark, bloody boil was quickly filling with pus where the comb had burned the skin, leaving behind the unmistakable impression of iron prongs.

"I'll put some more oil on it," Aunt Helen said. In a panic, she slathered more oil onto Hattie's head. It was exactly the wrong thing to do. The oil oozed over her already sensitive skin and into the burn. Hattie was screaming. Aunt Helen was not sure what to do, so she stood back in confusion, while Marlene rushed to

Hattie's side, and began barking orders.

"Helen, wet this towel and put it on her head. Doe, you and Pudge take some buckets down to the well. Fill one up with water and the other with mud. Hurry up!"

Marlene held Hattie's towel-wrapped head as gently as she could while the girl sobbed against her lap.

"Hattie, we got to get this stuff out yo' head," she said. "We gonna wash it out with soap. It's gonna hurt, but we'll do it as fast as we can, baby."

The next half hour was a pure ordeal for Hattie as they leaned her over the basin. She wouldn't let Helen near her head again, so Helen was tasked with holding her writhing body still while Marlene soaped her hair. As a last measure, Marlene plastered her entire head with cool mud.

Hattie was still in considerable pain and worn out with crying. Marlene sat with the frightened child in her lap. Uncle Roby brought her a cup to drink from. Marlene smelled the liquor. "We ain't got nothing else to give her for the pain," he said. "At least this might slow things down a little for her. Make her forget her hurts, maybe make her sleep."

Hattie's sobs had begun to subside, though her scalp still burned like crazy. She dutifully sipped the nasty liquor Uncle Roby had brought to her. "That's my good girl," he said, taking the cup from her with a smile. She mustered a smile in return. She took note of how extra nice everyone was being to her now that she was hurt.

Doe and Pudge voluntarily went back for more mud and water. Aunt Marlene cradled her in her arms and rocked her like a baby. And Uncle Roby, who never let anyone touch his bottle, was sharing his liquor with her.

Hattie could see Aunt Helen's distress. She kept pacing back and forth, exclaiming that it wasn't her fault that Hattie was so tender-headed, and that she never meant to burn the little girl. "She wouldn't sit still," she said.

"Helen, nobody thinks you burned that girl on purpose," Roby said. "Accidents happen." He looked to his wife.

"She gon' be alright?"

Marlene pursed her lips thoughtfully. "I got to see what her head looks like under this mud before it dries," she said. Then I'll see what we need to do."

What they needed to do turned out to be a trip up the road to Miz Sophie, an old black woman whom the children said was a witch. Miz Sophie mixed headache powders in some water and gave it to Hattie to drink for the pain. She cooled chamomile tea and used it to bathe Hattie's scalp. She plastered the girl's head with the wet leaves and wrapped it up in a rag.

Doe had taken a basket she'd been weaving and turned it into a straw hat for Hattie to wear over her scarf the next day. Aunt Helen donated a pink ribbon from her own fancy hat to wrap around the brim and, ever thoughtful, little Pudge picked some flowers to stick in it.

"You all saved me with your kindness that day," Hattie reminisced. The children had been warned not to reveal to anyone at church what had happened and Doe's beautiful hat concealed the ravages of Hattie's scalp and remaining hair. If the other women knew how Helen had burned Hattie during her hair-straightening process, they might be afraid to try it, and Helen needed their money. She had promised to share some of her profits with Marlene and Roby.

Doe had been relieved not to see Hattie subjected to any more humiliation. When the other kids admired Doe's shiny curls and asked why Hattie wasn't sporting some too, Doe defended her, saying that Hattie had been ordered not to take off her beautiful new hat.

Later that day, Hattie overheard Aunt Helen talking with Aunt Marlene and mama. She had said, "Lord, I hope that girl's head heals up soon. She ain't never gonna git no man like that."

Hattie looked now at Susan. Remembering her Aunt Helen, she thought about how beautiful everyone said that woman was, mainly because of her light skin. Susan probably thought you had to be light-skinned with long, straight hair in order to get a man, the same way Aunt Helen did. Well, she was wrong.

"Even you need to know I didn't get me just one man," Hattie said. Her voice sly with satisfaction. "All in all, I got me three." She sat back and looked at the two younger woman.

"Is that right, Mother Durham?" Susan said. "Are you going to tell us how you and Jerome's daddy met? I always wondered how you two got together."

"Maybe I will tell you, maybe I won't," Hattie sniffed. That Susan was just too eager, digging for dirt, probably. Hattie wasn't going to let her ruin a pleasant memory.

❧ Chapter Five ❧

The old woman recalled how she had continued to work at sewing and laundry with her Aunt Marlene, occasionally going home during odd weeks and weekends to spend time, at her mother's insistence, with her family. One weekend when she went home to find a young male stranger there. Hattie was shocked to be told the young man was to be her new husband.

"I was so surprised, Doe," Hattie told Lisa. "You and me had just been talking about boys and how we thought it would be to grow up and get married. But that was just talk. I wasn't ready for all that yet."

Ready or not, it was to be. Lewis Durham was the son of Bertha, one of Benton's cousins who lived up north. Lewis had gotten into some kind of trouble back home – exactly what he done was unknown, but it was bad enough that his mother had written to Benton, the only out-of-town relative she knew of, to ask if Lewis could come down South to live with the family and get out of harm's way. The family had pooled money together to send Lewis there. She had written her fervent hope that the boy would find a wife and settle down, and she hoped Benton and his relatives would help him do that.

With his eye on the money he knew Lewis had in his pocket, Benton was happy to oblige his cousin's request. His older daughters, Viola and Sharon, were both already married with children of their own. So he ordered his youngest daughter Hattie to gather her few things and get ready to move into the back shed house with the new arrival, unceremoniously giving his daughter, Hoot, to his cousin's wayward boy.

Hattie's mother did her best to save her daughter from a premature wedding night by insisting that the couple be properly married before living together. She asked Lewis to wait until that Sunday, when the minister could bless the union, before claiming his young wife. That would give her time to prepare her young daughter for marriage. The young couple would pay Benton rent to live in the shed.

That Sunday, Hattie wore the straw hat her cousin had made for her. She and Lewis went to church with the family where they were married by Reverend Pleasant. Since it was now Sunday and Hattie was due back at Aunt Marlene's to get back to work for the week, the young couple's wedding night was postponed by a week.

"I was some scared, Doe," Hattie said. "Thank goodness I had you to talk to about all that." The young girls had sat up late at night, whispering in the dark about what exactly it was that Hattie should expect on her wedding night. Her cousin knew of her fright, but what she didn't know was that Hattie also felt considerable relief and even some pride about the fact that she had gotten married before Dorothea, who everyone expected to be taken first because she was supposedly so beautiful.

Hattie knew other girls were jealous of her as well. Being from out of town made Lewis instantly desirable. As a northerner, he was assumed glamorous and sophisticated. He was a bit brash and his city ways would get him into more trouble if he wasn't careful. Benton and the other men would have their hands full trying to keep Lewis out of trouble in Alabama.

Hattie had initially been confused by the arrangement. It didn't shock her, though, that her father would find a way to get her out of his house again, for good this time, all while taking advantage of the situation. The rent he demanded in advance just about emptied Lewis Durham's wallet, and now the boy would go to work for the older man to pay off his debts. Hattie was surprised to find herself tied to this man, but she knew it could be worse.

Lewis was a strapping youth that drove women crazy with his brown skin, sparkling eyes, and even a gold tooth. The other girls her age commented on his good looks and she knew they were jealous of her good fortune in marrying this handsome man. Hattie was eager to please him. Hungry for the affection that marriage promised, she threw herself into the relationship and fancied herself in love.

For his part, Lewis didn't protest his imposed "marriage" too much. Hattie at 15 was a ripening young woman, and she belonged solely to him. She was tallish, with the kind of healthy hips and thighs that a man could enjoy. Though she had often been called ugly as a child, the dark-skinned young woman had grown into her features. The swollen bottom lip that looked exaggerated on her face as a child now formed a woman's full mouth. Grateful to have escaped the threat of death at home, Lewis thought he could put up with being a married man and work for his new father-in-law. Having someone else to order around made him the man of a house. If he ever got tired of his marital state, there was nothing stopping him from seeking his pleasure elsewhere. His situation was ideal, since Hattie worked for her aunt and had to be away from the house much of the time. She didn't need to know if he failed to come home or had company over some time.

When she was there, it was no hardship to be a husband to her. Hattie and Lewis were a healthy young couple, and there was no reason why they couldn't raise a family and be tolerably happy together. Hattie did her best. But by the time she gave birth to their second son, Hattie's devotion to Lewis had worn thin. "Marriage and motherhood took all my strength. Seemed like I didn't have any energy left for pleasure no more," lamented Hattie to no one in particular. She was in a daze now remembering what it had been like during those years.

The responsibilities of family life weighed on Lewis too. He and Hattie got along fairly well when he was sober, but the problem was he was increasingly drunk. He'd hit her a few times when he was in such a state. But sometimes Lewis became clumsy and found it difficult to focus his eyes when he'd been drinking, so often he'd just sit and stare at her in a stupor until he passed out. During those times, Hattie hated him the most. She wondered if she would ever escape her routine life and loveless marriage.

She didn't have to wonder long. Sewing and doing laundry alongside her Aunt Marlene exposed Hattie to many new things, especially since their work sometimes called for Hattie to go into town on errands or odd jobs. One day she received a message from one of the women she sometimes worked for stating that her sister needed a girl to come up for a few weeks to help with her wedding trousseau. It was the perfect opportunity for Hattie. She kissed little Carl and Lewis, Jr., goodbye, praying that their father would be responsible and take decent care of them while she was gone. Her mother and sisters would look in on them and make sure the family stayed fed and warm. She accepted a brief kiss on the cheek from Lewis, who stood there looking lost now that she would be gone for a while. She figured it was just a matter of time before he found his way into some trouble with alcohol, cards, and women, but that was not her worry now. Excited, she put on her pretty hat and got ready to go. She was ready for a new adventure and something good was bound to happen. She could feel it in her bones.

❧ CHAPTER SIX ❦

It was possible that Mother Durham wasn't going to be as big a problem as they had imagined, Susan thought. The old woman was obviously becoming unhinged. She was so delusional that she had been about to damage her own reputation by talking about her affair with a married man. All they had to do was convince people that Hattie really was crazy and that the she was making up her outrageous stories, of which she seemed to have an endless supply. Maybe she couldn't control her tongue. But maybe Susan and Jerome could make sure nobody believed anything the crazy old woman said.

There was no time to waste; she needed to get started. Jerome was busy with meetings that day, so Susan assured him she would stop by and make sure Mother Durham was doing all right.

Seeing how his mother trusted Lisa, Jerome had made the young woman a serious offer to come care for Hattie once they had selected a place for her. The facility where she was offered long-term care, but Jerome and Susan wanted something more private for his mother. No, they needed something more private for her, some place where she couldn't spill all her secrets to the public, and they needed it fast.

Now, Susan planned to use all of her persuasive skills to get Lisa to take the job. She sought Lisa out as soon as she got to the hospital, cornering her just before she entered Hattie's room.

"Lisa, I want to thank you so much for your kindness to my mother-in-law," Susan said. "She really seems to trust you."

"No need to thank me, Mrs. Durham," Lisa said. "I'm just doing my job."

"I'm sure listening to an old woman babble on forever is not a part of your job description," Susan said. "Wasn't that story she told us the other day the craziest thing you ever heard?" She watched the nurse carefully for her reaction. "I thought it was quite outlandish."

Lisa smiled politely. "I don't know if it was all that outlandish," she said. "Your mother-in-law was just remembering what it was like to be young and in love. Seems like she had so many struggles as a young girl, I was glad she found happiness with that man."

Lisa's words got Susan's mind spinning. Over the years, Jerome and his family had told mentioned several times how Hattie favored him over her other two sons. They all tried to justify it, saying that it was because Jerome was the youngest, the baby. But now, given the timing of what Hattie referred to as her "adventure" in town, Susan wondered if there wasn't something more to it.

She entered the room with Lisa and endured Hattie's customary scowl.

"Hello, Mother Durham," Susan said, rushing past Lisa to greet Hattie with an air kiss on the cheek.

"Where's Jerome?" Hattie demanded.

"You know how busy your son is," Susan said. "They had a council vote today, so I told him I would stop by."

"Well, I know you're busy too, baby," Hattie said.

"Lisa is here now, and she will take care of everything I need, so you can go." She waved her hand in a dismissive gesture and turned to her nurse. Susan held her tongue, sighed instead, and pulled a chair closer to Hattie's bed.

"Now, Mother Durham, I would like to stay," she said, taking Hattie's thin hand in her own. The old woman became stiff with suspicion.

"You and I have never spent much time together, and we don't know each other as well as we should," Susan continued. She patted Hattie's hand. "Now's our chance. Besides, you were telling us a great story the other day, and you didn't get to finish. I want to know what happened."

"What story?" Hattie grumbled. Lisa, busy arranging things on the night table, glanced over at her patient to make sure she was all right. Hattie was glowering, but there was curiosity in her eyes. The woman did love to talk. Susan was primed to take advantage of it.

"You were telling me and Miss Lisa here about the men in your life," she said.

"My men," Hattie said, nodding. "You mean my husband Lewis?"

"Yes, Lewis," Susan said reassuringly. Then, on a sudden instinct, she said, "And Raymond."

Hattie's eyes grew large, then she smiled and leaned back into her pillows. "Oh, yes, Raymond," she said, closing her eyes.

Susan kept patting Hattie's hand, hoping the repetitive motion would keep Mother Durham talking. Hattie was enjoying thinking about Raymond, who indeed had been the love of her life. As well as the reason for some terrible things she did, Hattie thought painfully. But she wasn't about to tell all that to her stuck-up daughter-in-law.

"You girls are young, but I'll tell you now, one thing I learned is that being in love can be dangerous. It will make you do anything and everything If you want to be with somebody bad enough," Hattie said. "Things you woulda never thought about doing before. Lord, have mercy."

Lisa continued about her work absentmindedly as she listened to the old woman talk.

"Things like what, Miss Hattie?" she said.

But Hattie fixed her gaze on Susan. "Like what I did to be with Raymond. Like what my Jerome did to be with you."

Susan paled beneath her makeup. "Mother Durham, I think you need some rest," she said hurriedly. To her relief, Hattie suddenly switched topics again.

"You know, I am feeling kind of tired now," she said. "Today they took me for a walk around this nice place you all done put me in. They got a nice little garden down there. What did you call it, baby?" She tugged Lisa's coat.

"The Chancelly Foster memorial garden," Lisa said. Susan froze again in shock. Watching her daughter-in-law's panicked reaction, Hattie smiled sweetly.

"Ain't that something, baby?" she said. "This is the hospital where they brought that boy, and his family donated a beautiful garden in his name after he died."

"Miss Hattie, why don't you close your eyes for a little while, and, when you're up to it, we'll get your dinner up here," Lisa intervened. "I'll check back in on you later."

"I'll give your love to Jerome and the kids, Mother Durham. He said he would stop by in the morning," Susan said cordially, hiding her panic. Susan leaned over coolly, giving her mother-in-law a brief goodbye kiss. Then she rushed out of the room ahead of Lisa, spinning on the young woman as she shut out the light in Hattie's room and entered the hall.

"What else did my mother-in-law tell you about Chancelly Foster?"

"Mrs. Durham, please," Lisa said. Susan Durham had rudely grabbed her. Susan removed her hand slowly from the nurse's shoulder and placed her face in her palms.

"I'm so sorry, Lisa, please forgive me. This family is under an incredible strain lately," she said. "The situation is terrible for my mother-in-law, getting so sick and confused all of a sudden. I just don't want anything to upset her, and I'm sure the name Chancelly Foster brought up some bad memories for her." She peeked over her lashes to see if Lisa was convinced.

"She did get a little upset," Lisa conceded, straightening her uniform. "Miss Hattie told me your family knew him."

"Yes, he and my husband were classmates," Susan said. "Did she tell you anything else?"

"Mrs. Durham, it really tore your mother-in-law up when she read the inscription in the garden," Lisa said. "It says 'In memory of Chancelly Foster, who gave his life saving another.'"

"I take it she told you why she found that so upsetting?" Susan persisted.

"Yes, ma'am. Miss Hattie confided in me that she was the reason that Chancelly Foster was a hero. She told me how hard it was telling everyone that she was the one he was trying to help when he took the fall that killed him."

Susan was visibly relieved. Hattie had stuck to the

same story she had told thirty years ago when Chancelly Foster had fallen to his death. The truth remained hidden, but how long before Hattie let it slip out, as she had with so many other things? Like the name Raymond. Susan still intended to find out exactly who he was.

"Poor Miss Hattie still feels responsible for what happened to Mr. Foster," Lisa was saying. "But after awhile she calmed down again. She said bygones were bygones and all she could do to make up for it now was to keep being as good and charitable as she could to others. And she's okay now, Mrs. Durham. I'm sorry about upsetting her."

"You couldn't have known about this family's past link to Chancelly Foster," Susan said, patting Lisa's hand reassuringly. "I'll just trust from now on that you all can find other places to take Mrs. Durham on her walk besides that memorial garden."

"Of course, Mrs. Durham," Lisa said. "Is your husband coming by to see her again soon?"

"He said he would stop by in the morning," Susan said.

She had made up her mind about a few things. One, Hattie needed to be moved as soon as possible, as far away from people and places that might trigger any more dangerous memories. Two, it would not do to hire Lisa as a private nurse for Hattie. She had grown too attached to the old woman. They needed someone who would do as they were told. But monitoring Hattie and keeping her under lock and key might not be enough to keep a lid on the old lady. Susan thought more drastic measures might be needed to prevent her mother-in-law from telling any more tales.

❧ Chapter Seven ❧

Somewhat shaken by her encounter with Susan Durham, Lisa stepped back into Hattie's room to check on her patient. To her surprise, Hattie was sitting up in her bed again.

"Mrs. Durham, I thought you were going to have yourself a little nap," she said.

"Come here, baby, I want to tell you something," Hattie coaxed. "I just wasn't gonna tell it while that damn daughter-in-law of mine was here, looking like a clown with all of that makeup on."

Lisa shook her head with amusement. Susan Durham had looked chic and flawless, the perfect woman to grace the arm of a handsome politician. "That suit she had on sure was nice," she said, trying to change the older woman's mood.

"Now, what is it, Mrs. Durham?" Lisa asked. She sat down in a chair by Hattie's bed. "What is it you want to tell me?"

"First, I want you to know I'm telling you because I think you'll understand," Hattie said. "After all, you and me got that in common. Just like me, you done something wrong because you was in love."

"What do you mean?"

"I mean, you committed a sin for love. Am I right?" She looked at Lisa closely. "You had a man that you loved, and you laid down with him even though the two of you weren't married."

"Yes, I guess so," Lisa blushed.

"You did it even though you knew it was a sin, because you also knew you loved that man and you planned to get married one day," Hattie persisted. "Well, that's what I did too. I laid down with a man who I wasn't married to. Maybe it was more wrong for me and my Raymond because we was both married to somebody else, but that didn't change the feeling we had. That didn't change the love."

"Mrs. Durham, you don't have to tell me all of that business," Lisa protested.

"No, now, Doe, I want to tell it," Hattie said, and Lisa realized the old woman had forgotten who she was talking to again. As she had done before, she had slipped into the past and thought she was conversing with her cousin.

"I met Raymond in town that year when I went to work for Miz Ammons," she said. "Oh, yes, girl, that Miz Ammons worked us hard trying to get ready for her daughter's wedding. She would send me into town to buy thread and such, and I was always glad to go just to have a chance to get away. And I would walk the long way around by that lumber yard so I could have a little more time to myself, and that's where I first saw Raymond."

Hattie recalled that the air near the lumber yard was fragrant with the scent of newly-cut wood and was filled with the sound of men yelling congenially to one another. Their voices made a pleasant contrast to the shrill sound of the Ammons' women's constant demands.

Hattie smiled, remembering how the big man with the golden skin and soft curly hair would wave to her and walk over to the fence to engage her in conversation. She had felt shy around him at first. He was so tall and so good looking. But he was friendly – and talkative too – and soon put her at her ease. One day he jumped over the fence and offered to walk with her a little way up the road. He had a bottle of soda. To her surprise, he took out another one and handed it to her.

"My name's Raymond. Raymond Peace," he said with a formal nod.

"Mine's Hattie," she said shyly. She didn't offer her last name, knowing how easy it was for people to find out things about you.

"You're not from around here, are you, Hattie?" Raymond said. "At least, I never saw you before this summer."

Hattie's soft accent reminded him of back home. He had been raised the only male in a houseful of doting women who talked in that same sweet soft way that she had. Hattie stole shy glances at what was surely the most handsome man she had ever seen. Raymond Peace stood six feet and four inches tall. His mother's people were folks most recently up from the Carolinas; His father was full-blooded Creek Indian. Raymond's facial features were finely carved. His most distinguishing features were his eyes, which were a clear, dark gold color, and his big, cleft chin that ended with a dimple just below his lower lip.

Hattie chuckled to herself thinking about how that man used to flatter her. Raymond said her dark skin was cool and beautiful, like a shady spot on a hot, sunny day. He told her that the way she wrapped her head made her look like a queen, and he liked her easy temperament too.

When Hattie asked him why he was so interested in her, he said he couldn't quite explain the feeling that drew him to her. Since he'd gotten married, he hadn't been with other women. He told Hattie that his Lullah was a good wife and a good mother to his kids, though she did put on airs sometimes. Hattie nodded. All the light skinned women she knew did that, as if they thought extra pretty manners put them a step closer to being white. Lullah Peace was certainly halfway there, as she was supposedly the daughter of the white man who owned the lumber yard where Raymond worked.

Luke Cooper had handpicked the handsome, hardworking foreman for his daughter, knowing that she would be well taken care of. Steadfast, reliable Raymond enjoyed the highest position and many privileges at the lumberyard, which was why he had the time and freedom to drum up a conversation with Hattie and get to know her. Hattie felt their arranged marriages gave her and Raymond something else in common. They had both been selected for their spouses, not chosen them on their own. She fell head over heels in love.

"Raymond made me feel things I ain't never felt in all the time I was with my husband, Lewis," Hattie said. "That's how I knew it was love. I also knew something else."

"Raymond put his baby in me the first time we got together. I knew it. I could feel it," Hattie said. "All those years I been putting that powder I got from Miz Sophie in a drink to help keep me from having any babies, but I guess Raymond Peace's manhood was too strong. Miz Sophie always told me it didn't work sometimes, but it seems like it worked fine until me and Raymond got together," Hattie sighed. "Then I knew what I had to do."

CHAPTER EIGHT

H attie had set to work seducing Lewis as soon as she could, as often as she could, to ensure the belief that he was the father of their expected child. If Lewis had any suspicion over his wife conceiving ten years after their last child had been born, he buried it under his vain pride in still being able to get a woman pregnant after all this time Not that he should have had any doubts; Lewis Durham was suspected to have fathered more than a few bastards around town.

"I bet you think that's scandalous," Hattie told Lisa. "Believe me, I wanted to shout to the world that I was gonna have a baby for Raymond Peace. But I had to let everybody think Jerome was Lewis' baby so as not to bring shame on the family."

The more Hattie had thought about it, the more she had wanted to find another way to live and be happy. Now that she had found real love, the prospect of spending a lifetime with Lewis Durham felt like a prison sentence. So far she had kept the truth from Raymond, but she decided to tell him he had fathered the child growing inside of her. Hattie found herself fantasizing often about what it would be like to be married to Raymond or even just to be able to near him all of the time. She wondered if maybe she could find a place for her and her boys to live in town, where she and Raymond could get together more often. She tried to see herself in an arrangement like the ones her father had with various women over the years: visiting, bringing money and food when he could, and living with them sometimes for days or weeks at a time.

Hattie wasn't sure about all of that, but Raymond had said he loved her, so she felt confident that he would help figure out a way for them to be together.

But Hattie was in for a surprise when she walked over to the lumber yard that day. Raymond was nowhere to be found. His co-workers informed her that Luke Cooper was opening up a yard in Montgomery, and he had sent Raymond ahead to get operations started. They weren't sure when he was coming back. Hattie's mind reeled in shock and disbelief as she labored her way home that day. She didn't know when Raymond was coming back, and she wasn't sure what her next move would be. Hattie supposed she was destined to play things out with Lewis, their two sons together, and the baby he thought belonged to him. But Hattie was in for another shock.

That night after she put the boys to bed, there was a knock on the door.

"Two of Lewis' friends brought him home that night, dragging him between them," she recalled. "Somebody had beaten Lewis half to death. The man was black, blue, and bloody. I didn't even recognize him, they beat him so bad."

Shocked, she had opened the door and stepped out of the way so they could bring Lewis in. He could not stand on his own, so the two men supported him on either side as Hattie stared at him in disbelief.

"Do you think he's going to die?" Hattie was frightened out of her wits. She couldn't imagine any man surviving a beating like the one Lewis had taken.

"Nah," said Vernon. "But he's beat up bad, and he's going to need some good care. He might have some broken ribs. You need to wrap him up good to hold 'em place, but you got to be careful not to poke him through his lungs. He's having some trouble breathing already because his nose is all busted up."

"They busted up his teeth pretty good, too," Milton added. "Wash his mouth out real good to make sure that bleeding ain't coming from his insides. If not, chances are pretty good that he's going to make it. Healing up is gonna take some some time. He ain't going to be able to work or nothing for a while."

Hattie thanked the men for bringing her husband home. She asked them to stay long enough to hold him up while she poured a couple of pails of water over him.

"Stop that, Hoot! It's cold," Lewis cried out, moaning in pain.

"I got to do this, Lewis," she said. She hated him for calling her by that ugly name, Hoot. "I got to clean you up so I can see what I got to deal with here."

The men laid Lewis on the bed and left hurriedly, embarrassed to see their fellow cohort in such a condition. Hattie stared at the man on the bed in revulsion. Lewis was funky with the combined odors of sex, smoke, and alcohol and all the other nasty smells conjured after a night of fear, pain, and fighting. His face was so swollen he was barely recognizable. Sure enough, he was missing several teeth, including the shiny gold one that made him so popular with fancy women. Hattie was sure that the only thing keeping Lewis from feeling worse pain was the fact that he was so drunk.

She brought an empty bucket over for him to use and set to work on his wounds, cleaning him up the best she could. He had half fallen asleep as she tried to sit him up and wrap him up in a sheet she had torn up to bandage his ribs. He made a horrible, gurgling snore, struggling to breathe through busted ribs and a broken nose.

Hattie sat down next to the bed and tried to think. Her husband wasn't just a problem for now. What about the days ahead? The family would have to get by as he slowly healed, since a man with broken bones and god knew what other injuries would not be able to work. She wouldn't be able to work herself as long as he required care. She sighed. Being married to a man like Lewis was bad enough; being married to an injured Lewis would be a nightmare. Hattie panicked as she realized that the hours it would take nursing Lewis were precious hours that would also be stolen from her and Raymond.

On the other hand, without Lewis, she would be free to be with Raymond. She could take the boys and maybe move to town, work more hours for the Ammons sisters and be closer to Raymond. If she was free, maybe he would even move in with her. At the very least, he would be able to spend more time with her, maintaining a second family with her the same way her father had done with his women on the side.

She helped Lewis lay back and observed her work. She had done a good job cleaning him up, considering the sorry state he was in. She had helped him rinse his mouth out several times till the water ran nearly clear and had gently, firmly wrapped his ribs. He was badly bruised and likely had some fractured and broken bones, but under his blanket he was clean and naked except for his bandages. Whoever had beaten Lewis Durham had tried to kill him. What if they found out he was not dead? Were they angry enough to come back and try to finish what they had started? Hattie felt her panic growing worse, simmering into anger as she thought about it. She knew the meanness of people, had seen what anger and spite could make them do. She remembered being a little girl and how her slip of the tongue telling people her family was rich had brought the wrath of an angry group of violent white men down on her house. If the men who had beaten Lewis came after him and found his family there too their innocence might not be enough to save them.

Lewis was still gurgling and snoring. Breathing was clearly a difficult task for him. She didn't think he would be able to do so easily, or even walk right, again. Was it a sign?

Whether it was or not, Hattie saw her chance. She raised the wadded-up bundle of bloody rags over the face of her sleeping husband. He coughed and mumbled her name. She lowered the bundle and held it there until his weak struggles ceased.

CHAPTER NINE

Lisa had difficulty concealing her shock at the old woman's words. In all her years as a nurse, she had seen and heard many things, but nothing as shocking and distressing as this. What had started out as a confession of a foolish affair with a married man had turned into an admission of murder. Mrs. Durham was visibly distraught as the unpleasant memory came flooding back. She was trembling and seemed on the verge of tears as she demanded, "You can see why I did that, baby, can't you?"

"Lewis couldn't have lived after all that," she continued. "He was hurt too bad. I didn't think he could work or even walk again, and I don't know how we was gonna feed our boys with neither of us working, let alone take care of a new baby.

"Besides, with all his teeth gone, Lewis wasn't pretty no more," she rambled on. "His pride couldn't have took that, not able to work and the teeth he was so proud of all busted up. Shoot, Lewis was already an angry man. He would have been impossible to live with after all that. He woulda just took it out on me and my boys," said Hattie, seeming to justify her actions to herself. "It was a hard thing to do, but I think I did the right thing by him and by everybody else, too."

Hattie looked carefully at Lisa.

"You a nurse," she said. "So you know what it is trying

to fix people. And you know what it is trying to help people who can't be fixed. Lewis was like that. He could not be fixed," she said firmly. "I just tried to help him feel better as best as I could, and then I helped him on to the next life, just a little quicker than he would have moved on otherwise. That's all."

"Oh, Mrs. Durham," was all Lisa could manage to say. She patted the old woman's hand, trying to comfort her. Hattie was nodding and mumbling to herself, seeming to work through her emotions. When she looked up again, her expression was calm.

"I know you think it's a scandal, me putting Lewis Durham out of his sorry misery like that," she said. "But that ain't all I done. To me, Raymond Peace was a gift from heaven, and he was my man in ways that my husband never was." Hattie nodded with determination. "When it comes down to your man, you do whatever you have to do to keep him. So, yes, I have had to kill for the man I loved, and I was ready to do it again."

Lisa was still trying to fathom the old woman's words, but Hattie seemed satisfied with her justifications.

"I think God can forgive me for what happened to Lewis Durham, because he seen all the bad things that man done to me," Hattie said. "But I ain't never meant to kill no baby!"

Now the old woman's bottom lip was trembling, and she had grown agitated. Lisa had never seen anyone else whose moods changed so quickly. Now Hattie was in tears again, sobbing incoherently about a baby. Lisa got to work adjusting Hattie's pillows and IV cart, hoping to calm the patient down. She thought maybe Hattie was about to confess now to getting rid of an unwanted child. As a woman, Lisa knew that was a problem many women faced at some time or other in their lifetimes. The procedures were illegal and dangerous, and no one would go through such a thing unless they felt they had to. Lisa had also seen many women hospitalized because of the abusive men in their lives. It sounded like Hattie Durham had certainly faced her share of troubles.

"Mrs. Durham, try to calm down and get some sleep now," Lisa said. "You've told me enough for one night. You don't have to talk about this anymore."

The medicine she had injected into Hattie's IV had already started to do its work. The old woman had started to grow quiet. She folded her arms and shook her shoulders, trying to get settled as she began to fall asleep. But the medicinal fog that enveloped her sleep soon gave way to dreams. The ghosts in Hattie's past pushed her back into her memories. As Hattie slept, she slipped back into a troubled dream of her past.

Not long after Lewis died, Hattie had given birth to the beautiful baby boy she named Jerome. He looked nothing like her other children, but had inherited many of his father's fine features. Jerome had dark curly hair and golden brown skin. It tickled Hattie to hear her late husband's relatives trying to take credit for Jerome's good looks. She would duck her head and nod as they cited this or that uncle with skin that particular shade, a similar grade of hair, or a big, handsome chin like that.

Jerome was a constant reminder of his father, and Hattie found herself thinking constantly of Raymond. She longed to be with him again, touching his skin and watching him smile. Wherever he was, she just knew that he felt the same way. Now, with Lewis gone, Hattie felt sure she could convince Raymond to leave his wife and move in with her. Hadn't he said he loved her?

Feeling sorry for the young widow, people were still bringing food and other necessities by the house, offering to run errands and do favors for her. Hattie knew she had to move fast while she had a chance. She got her sisters and cousins to agree to look after the children for a few days. The two older boys, Carl and Lewis, Jr., were big enough to do a lot for themselves, but they still needed meals and some supervision, while baby Jerome needed constant care. That was no problem as the women in the family constantly competed with one another over who should hold Jerome, or feed him, or bounce him to sleep. The baby boy charmed everyone.

Hattie hitched a ride into town and made several stops. First, she went by the Ammons house to see if the family was willing to take her on again now that she'd had the baby. The next stop was Miz Sophie's house to obtain more of the healer's mysterious herb powder that had effectively prevented previous pregnancies. Hattie was sure she and Raymond would be making love again as soon as he saw her. The thought thrilled her to near delirium. How she loved that man. Hattie shyly asked Miz Sophie if it were possible to get a stronger dose of her famous birth control powder, since it apparently had not been enough to stop Raymond's seed from taking before.

Miz Sophie had gone back into her pantry and brought back a small bag filled with a different, darker powder. She warned Hattie that the medicine was extremely potent and must be taken carefully, in small, precise doses and at the right time of day in order to work properly. "Too much will kill you, and too little will make you sick, but it won't stop no babies if you don't take enough," Miz Sophie had said. "You got to measure it just right."

Now, properly equipped, Hattie made a beeline to her third stop, the lumber yard. Her heart was pounding in anticipation. Would Raymond be there? To her disappointment, he was not. The man she had talked to before – who was acting as foreman in Raymond's absence – explained that Raymond had been back but was now gone again on another trip for the owner. Hattie hid her disappointment.

"Did his wife go with him?" she asked. She had badly wanted to see Raymond, but a different possibility suddenly occurred to her. Meanwhile, the man was laughing.

"No ma'am," he said. "Miss Lullah ain't hardly trying to go on no trip with a houseful of babies."

Hattie hid her relief and asked where the Peace's lived. Raymond was away, and his wife, Lullah, was home alone with her children. An idea had begun to form in Hattie's mind. She was curious about her rival, the half-white woman who wore her Raymond's ring.

She was surprised as she approached the house. It was much bigger than she had expected. She checked the number to make sure it was the right place, and it was. A woman was struggling to drag a tub of wet clothes down the steps. Was that Raymond's wife?

Lullah Peace was a red-boned woman, larger than Hattie had expected. She had imagined a petite little thing, but Lullah was big and healthy, with pink freckled skin and thick reddish hair that sprung out of a messy bun at the nape of her neck. She was sweating as she heaved the tub down another step.

"Let me help you with that," Hattie called as she ran up to lend a hand, thinking a girl like that should have no problem with a little tub of laundry.

"Thank you," the woman said. "If you'll just grab hold of that other side there, we're just going to walk it down to the clothesline."

"You Lullah? I'm Hattie," Hattie offered as they sat the tub down. Lullah put her hand in the small of her back and stretched.

"Oh, my Lord," she said. "Things just seem to get heavier and heavier around here. My back is killing me. I have to sit down."

As Hattie followed her back to the house, she turned and said, "I sure don't mean to be rude, but today I got a backache and a headache. It must be my day for aches." She sat back down on the steps.

"Now, to answer your question, yes, I'm Lullah. Mrs. Raymond Peace," Lullah added proudly. "And you are?"

"My name is Hattie," answered Hattie, not sure she wanted to give her last name or not. "I'm a friend of your husband, Raymond. We met down at the lumber yard."

Lullah's eyebrow went up. "No women working at the lumber yard."

Hearing the suspicion in Lullah's voice, Hattie hurried to reassure her.

"No, ma'am, I don't work there," she said. "I work for the Ammons family downtown. You know them?" When Lullah didn't answer, Hattie went on.

"They send me on errands down by the yard all the time. One day I was walking by there, and it was so hot,

I was about to faint. Your Raymond saw me and knew I was doing poorly, so he brought me a block to sit on and some cool water. He is a real gentleman."

"That is true." Lullah beamed at hearing her husband praised.

"We been pretty nice friends ever since," Hattie said innocently. "And ever since then, I been telling myself I got to do something for that man to show how thankful I am for him being so nice to me. I went looking for him today at the lumber yard and they told me Raymond was gone." Hattie could see how her statement rekindled Lullah's suspicions. She was wondering what kind of brazen girl would go looking for her husband, a married man, at his job. Hattie smiled reassuringly.

"Now, when I found that Raymond was out of town, I thought to myself, well, here's my chance," she said. "I can go and help his wife out for a little while, and that would be a way to return all his kindness to me. I think he would appreciate it, you being alone here with your kids and all."

Lullah was still skeptical, but she was grateful for the help. She was a strong woman and usually had no problem taking care of her home and her children, but she had been feeling poorly these last couple of days. The children needed to be bathed and fed, and this Hattie person seemed kind and sincere. She was also effective and quick, heating up their supper, putting together the pie Lullah had rolled out the dough for but hadn't finished, and getting the children squared away. Raymond's little boy and girl were miniature split images of their father and mother.

Hattie fixed Lullah some warm milk and had her put

her feet up while Hattie cleaned up the dinner dishes and put away the clothes she had helped fold. She let herself out, leaving Lullah dozing in a chair. Once outside Hattie stopped to break off a big branch and filled her pocket with rocks. There were many things a black woman walking alone in the dark through Lowndes County should fear under those circumstances. But along with her nerves and fear, Hattie admitted to feeling something else. She felt positively exhilarated. She had done what she had set out to do, and that hadn't been all that hard at all. Waiting would be harder, but it would be worth it. Raymond might be sad at first, but Hattie had no doubt in her ability to comfort him. Hadn't he said that her touch was soft and sweet enough to make a man forget anything? Hattie giggled with delight, thinking about how she would prove he was right. Thoughts of making love with Raymond occupied her mind and she forgot her fears on that long walk home in the dark.

ಬ CHAPTER TEN ೦೪

The two days' wait had seemed like an eternity, but Hattie held her peace. She tended patiently to her boys and responded sweetly to family and friends inquiring after her health. After all, she was supposed to be a grieving widow who had just given birth to boot. Hattie kept her face down and her voice low, hoping no one would suspect her true feelings. No one could know her joy at finally being free of that abusive, no-count husband of hers. And no one could know about the fine man she already had in mind to take Lewis' place. But now, soon, Raymond would be free too. She would tell him about the beautiful son they had together, and he would put his gold band on her finger. She didn't think they would want to stay in the county, but they would make a wonderful life somewhere together. She could barely wait.

Once again, Hattie talked the family into watching her boys. She took special care with her dress and headwrap, and hitched a ride into town. She looked for Raymond at the lumber yard and encountered the same man who had told her Raymond's whereabouts before. This time Pete Hurley's voice was mournful.

"Yes, Mr. Peace is back in town, but he ain't at work today," he said. "They done had a death in the family."

"Oh, no," said Hattie, hoping she sounded genuinely surprised. "May I ask who passed?"

"They say Miss Lullah done lost a baby," the man answered. "A baby boy, I hear. "

Hattie felt like her own heart had stopped. She didn't hear her own sharp intake of breath or feel herself stumble a few steps back. The man reached for her arm to steady her.

"Oh, my Lord," Hattie said. "Have mercy."

"You all right, ma'am? It is a tragedy," the man responded. "No one likes to bear that kind of bad news, but you asked me to tell."

"I didn't know she was expecting," Hattie said out loud to herself. "I didn't know."

"Sometimes His ways are mysterious," the man said respectfully, startling Hattie. She had forgotten he was standing there.

"So, Mrs. Peace is all right then?" she asked, staring at him. He drew in a long breath.

"I hear she's taking it hard, but she seems to have pulled through the worst of it," he replied.

Hattie couldn't wait a moment longer. She thanked him hastily for his help and headed down the road toward Raymond's house. As she walked, her mind was a wild jumble. Lullah Peace was alive. And in her place an innocent soul had departed this world before even setting a foot in it. Because of me, Hattie thought. She could not yet bring herself to face the facts. But this was what Miz Sophie's strong medicine could do. It could stop a baby from being born, as it was meant to do. Too much of it could kill a grown person, as Hattie had meant for it to do. Instead, now an innocent baby – a baby boy! – had been robbed of life. "I didn't know she was expecting," Hattie murmured again as she rushed to find Raymond.

He was sitting outside on the steps in the same place where she had first seen his wife struggling with her tub of wash. Raymond was just sitting there. His face was bleak. He stood up as he saw Hattie approach. Her walk turned into a run.

Hattie rushed up to Raymond and threw her arms around him.

"You been gone so long, I didn't think I would see you again," she said, snuggling her face into his chest. After standing there for a moment, Hattie realized he wasn't returning her embrace.

"I'm sure you didn't hear," she went on, "But my husband Lewis passed." She waited for his reaction.

"I sure am sorry to hear about that, Hattie," Raymond said. He sounded sincere, though his voice sounded stiff. "I hope you and your boys are making out okay."

"We been all right," Hattie said. "You know I got my people and Lewis' people helping out," she said. "We're gonna be all right, praise the Lord."

"But what about you, Raymond?" Hattie knew she had to approach the subject carefully. "I heard tell your Lullah took sick?"

"She did, real bad sick, but she's going to be okay," Raymond replied. His voice was cold, so cold Hattie actually shivered.

"Is that right? Praise the Lord," said Hattie, her voice trailing off at the end. This was not the news she had wanted to hear about Raymond's wife. Raymond was watching Hattie's reaction closely.

"That's right, Hattie. My wife is going to be all right," he said. "But she lost our baby."

"What are you talking about, Raymond?" she said,

struggling to sound surprised. Raymond started to pace, his voice breaking.

"I'm talking about my wife, Hattie. Whatever made Lullah so sick also made her miscarry. A boy. He came too early."

"I didn't know your wife was expecting," Hattie said feebly. Her mind was reeling.

"Lullah thinks she must have eaten something to make her push our baby out too soon," he said. He fought back his tears. "That's what she said it felt like."

Hattie's mind kept repeating the awful thought. Raymond's wife was alive – sick but alive – and not going anywhere soon. Raymond looked at her hard, and then he started shaking her.

"What did you do, Hattie?" he demanded. "Lullah told me you came to see her."

"I wanted to help her out," Hattie tried to explain, but Raymond was growing furious.

"She told me you cooked some food in my kitchen," Raymond said. "What else did you do, Hattie?"

"I just stirred the stew and made up some cornbread and helped her finish rolling out the dough to make the pie she couldn't finish cause the kids was acting up," Hattie said frantically. She thought she saw a way out.

"Lullah even invited me to join the family for dinner, and we all sat down and ate together," she said. "Me and your wife and your sweet little Albertina and that handsome son of yours, Raymond, Jr. We all ate some of that food, and none of the rest of us got sick ... that I know of. Are your little girl and boy all right?"

"Dammit, Hattie," said Raymond, ignoring her question. He started to circle her slowly. "Lullah told me you fixed her something warm to drink after y'all ate."

"Oh, yes, I heated up some milk with chamomile in it to help her rest. That girl seemed so tired running after the children and all."

"You put something in Lullah's tea, didn't you, Hattie?" Raymond said wearily. It was more of a statement than a question. Seeing the pain in Raymond's eyes caused Hattie to go numb.

"I didn't know she was expecting," she said feebly.

"Nobody did. She didn't even know herself until it was too late," Raymond said. "The baby's gone, but my wife is going to live, that is, if the grief don't kill her."

"I thought you and me was gonna be together," Hattie started to explain. "Lewis passed and left me alone with my boys and my own new baby, and I figured you and me would be together."

"I never promised you that, Hattie," Raymond said sadly.

Speaking her fantasy out loud made Hattie realize how ridiculous it actually sounded. It was like a light suddenly came on, and she saw the truth for what it was. Raymond was never going to leave Lullah for her, especially now. He knew what she had done, or tried to do, and his innocent unborn child was dead. Would he ever be able to forgive her?

Raymond was shaking his head now and Hattie could feel him withdrawing slowly from her. His amber eyes were dark with sorrow and something else that caused Hattie to recoil. It was anger.

"The milk didn't kill her, but the grief just might," he said. "Go home, Hattie."

"Raymond," she began, but he was pulling away.

"You know my boss is Lullah's daddy, don't you," he said. Hattie nodded. She had heard. It was no big deal knowing that a rich white man had fathered Lullah, but his attitude toward his colored daughter was a bit of a surprise. The man didn't even try to hide their relationship. On the contrary, everybody knew how he spoiled and doted on the young woman.

"He's fond of her," Raymond said woodenly. "No telling what he might do if he thought somebody intentionally meant to hurt her."

"I didn't know she was expecting," Hattie repeated again, stupidly. Raymond looked at her for a minute, growing visibly more disgusted at the sight.

"Get on home while you still can before somebody starts asking questions," he said. "Go on."

Watching Raymond back away, Hattie suddenly felt the awful truth of what she had done. It was like a kick in the gut. She had actually tried to murder a woman and had killed her lover's baby instead. What could make her do something horrible like that?

She had heard that having a baby could sometimes make a woman go stone crazy. Was that what had happened to her after birthing Jerome? It must have for her to think she could force Raymond to be with her. It must have to make her try commit a sin like murder. The sin had been committed. Instead of Lullah Peace, Hattie's victim was an innocent child.

❧ CHAPTER ELEVEN ❧

I n the days and months afterward, Hattie had lived in a fog of depression that worried her family. They had no knowledge of what her true troubles were and chalked it up to the fact that she was a recent widow and struggling single mother. It was enough to take a body down. But enough people cared about Hattie to gather around her and help her the best they could, and soon she started to come out of it.

The somber woman immersed herself in her church and her Bible. Hattie imagined her penance was in Raymond's absence from her life, since having him with her was the reason she had committed such unthinkable sins. She didn't think she would ever see him again, but couldn't help hoping that someday Raymond would learn about Jerome. In the meantime, she was sure that the only way to atone for her sins was to devote herself completely to children and to the Lord. Hattie did not know if she could ever find forgiveness, but she certainly meant to try.

Hattie became the example of Christian charity at the church. She was especially devoted to children and worked extra hard helping out at church events to collect food, clothing, and toys for children. Everyone was fond of the widow Durham, who always had time to change a diaper or wash a skinned knee. She always said, "Every child deserves to be loved," and her children's peers, especially young girls, often went to Hattie with their troubles.

Everyone knew how much she loved her sons. As hard as it was not to show favoritism to Jerome, Hattie gave it her best effort. Still she knew her preference for her youngest son was obvious to everyone. Jerome was a handsome child who had inherited more than just his father's physical appeal. Jerome worked hard and was always eager to please. He was always talking about wanting to help people. If Raymond could only see his son, Hattie thought, he would be so proud. Maybe he could forgive me.

Hattie thought she had to be doing something right. Whatever the case, her luck held and even thrived. After initially balking at the "likely accidental" cause of Lewis Durham's death, the couple of two-bit insurance policies he held eventually paid out. The money was enough to make up for the loss of his income and then some. Hattie was able to save up, get ahead some, and, later, even pay for some schooling for the boys.

All three of her sons were healthy, loyal, and smart, though Jerome continued to be the apple of everyone's eye. And it seemed Raymond had kept his wife from going to her father with any suspicions about Hattie's visit. At least, no one had come around looking to hurt her the way she had once feared vindictive people might come to harm Lewis. Not yet, anyway. Still, Hattie was nervous and took the step of moving another county over. It didn't hurt to put distance between her family and potential trouble. Still, she liked to think Raymond's discretion showed he still had a soft spot in his heart for her. Maybe someday her dreams would come true, and they would meet again. Raymond would realize that she had not only acted out of desperation, but that she had acted out of real, true love. It never hurt to hope.

Ten years passed. Life settled into a routine as Hattie continued to work hard with her church and supporting the school that was in her community. So when Mr. Woods – the elementary teacher at the school – was transferred to another school, Hattie, along with other members of the community, was interested in learning who the school board would hire for the position. It didn't take long to hear that another teacher had been hired. Many of the church members were whispering that it was a woman. Not only that, she was young and single. Curiosity rose to a fever pitch.

It wasn't long before the new teacher moved to town. Everyone wanted to know more about the apparently bright young lady. Hattie was going to get that opportunity this Sunday.

That Sunday morning, Reverend Jackson gave the usual energetic sermon, preaching hard about not giving in to various temptations. Hattie felt her face heat up with shame, recalling how easily she had given in to temptation with Raymond. All that was behind her now, though she still thought about him often.

Before dismissing the congregation, Reverend Jackson said he had a special announcement to make. "On behalf of the Holy Redeemer Church family, I would like to extend a special welcome to a new arrival in town. This young lady will be teaching the children at the elementary, and although I know we will all miss Mr. Woods," Reverend Jackson paused dramatically, then looked around with a broad smile, "we are happy to welcome our new teacher, Miss Peace, to our community."

The moment Hattie heard the name, she felt her heart stop. Peace was not a common last name. Reverend Jackson was grinning broadly. "Please come and stand by me, Albertina."

Now Hattie felt true panic. Wasn't Albertina the name of Raymond's daughter? Other church members had immediately started to introduce themselves to the beautiful young woman.

Hattie waited her turn, grateful for the time it took for her heart to start beating at a normal pace. When the time came, she asked Miss Peace to tell something of herself. The young woman with the tea-brown skin and dark, reddish hair pulled into a neat bun smiled and stated she was from a small town in Lowndes County.

"Is that right?" Hattie responded. She did not share the fact that she was from Lowndes too and hoped that there would be no occasion for Albertina to find that information out. Hattie bristled as the talkative girl stated that she was the oldest child of Raymond and Lullah Peace from Hayneville, Alabama. Albertina's diction was perfect and proper, as a young, well-raised schoolteacher's should be.

As Albertina talked, Hattie noted the girl's resemblance to her mother, Lullah. She was stunned by the rush of emotion that flooded through her. Though she knew it was wrong, Hattie's jealousy was as fresh as it had been years ago. Lullah Peace had done nothing to deserve a man like Raymond, besides be born half-white, spoiled, and lucky enough to survive poisoning. Hattie felt her resentment growing and found herself taking it out on Albertina.

She often found herself working with the young lady at the school, and her tone was always sharp when she spoke to the girl. Poor Albertina was puzzled by the older woman's attitude towards her. Mrs. Durham had seemed so friendly and interested at first, but now she behaved as if she could barely tolerate the young woman. Still, Albertina remained courteous and respectful, as she had always been taught to do.

Hattie's coldness to Albertina Peace did not have the desired effect. She had thought to hurt the girl, but Albertina maintained her composure, or seemed to. Hattie found her enmity growing. In Hattie's mind, Albertina represented the reason Raymond had left her. To Hattie, Albertina was Lullah. Spiraling downward into hatred, Hattie made up her mind to get revenge.

One afternoon, Albertina stayed late at the school to finish up some work. Hattie passed the school and Albertina saw her through the windows. She waved and hollered a greeting, but Hattie would not acknowledge the friendly gesture. Instead she rushed ahead, trying to get to the store before it closed. She quickly grabbed the items that she need and headed out the door. As she headed back toward the school, she noticed that the lights were still on in Miss Peace's classroom.

Hanging around on the side of the building was Sam Tate. Thick through the shoulders, with a mean, bulldog face, Sam was known around town as a low-class man who stayed in trouble.

He called to Hattie, "Hey there, Hattie, how you?"

Hattie replied, "Doing fine." She kept walking, wanting nothing to do with the likes of Sam Tate. But Sam followed her.

"That a nice-looking new woman y'all got working down at the school now," he persisted, fishing for information. A fresh female was always a topic of interest to a man like him. As he spoke, an idea popped into Hattie's head.

"Yes, she pretty and all, but I heard she has been with lots of men," she said.

"Oh, yeah?" Sam said. He grinned. "She don't care who it is?"

"Some women are just like that, I guess," Hattie shrugged. She knew that if she planted a seed in Sam's head, he would try to take advantage of it.

"Take care, Sam, I got things to do," said Hattie, continuing on her way. Just as she had thought, Sam decided to go to the school to get a little of the action that Hattie had implied Albertina was giving out. But instead of going to the store as she had intended, Hattie waited for Sam to turn around and slink back to the school. She followed him. There was more to her plan, and no part of it involved letting him have his way with Albertina Peace.

Careful not to be seen, Hattie stood outside the classroom door that Sam had entered. She heard Sam and Albertina talking inside. She could not make out the specific words, but the tone of their voices was easy to follow. First, the conversation was polite. Then, Sam's tone became rough, while Albertina sounded panicked. Hattie held her breath, waiting for just the right time.

The sounds of a struggle could be heard. Albertina was a large girl, built like her mother, but she was not able to defend herself alone against the stronger, heavier Sam Tate. He easily overcame her, forcing her up against a wall. Albertina screamed.

Just then, Hattie entered the room. "Sam Tate, get away from that girl," she commanded. Sam could not believe his eyes. Hattie had been the one who sent him here, for God's sake.

"Go on and mind your business, Hattie, like you said you was gonna do," he snarled. "Me and this girl got business here."

"You have no business here at all, Tate," Hattie said. "Let her go now, and we won't say nothing to the police about how you tried to force yourself on a helpless woman."

Sam pushed Albertina away with a frustrated snarl. The girl ran sobbing from the room as he zipped up his pants and walked away, grumbling. Hattie smiled to herself. Things had gone exactly as she had hoped they would, although Sam had gone too far in grabbing Albertina the way he had. She hoped the girl was not too badly hurt. If things went the way she had hoped, she and Raymond Peace might be reunited soon.

The next day, Hattie listened with interest to the news that Albertina Peace had suddenly quit her new job teaching at the school. Hattie imagined that Raymond might come up there soon, looking to settle with whomever had tried to violate his daughter. Hattie allowed herself to fantasize freely about running into him. He would be as handsome as ever, and he would tell her she was still the same dark, cool-shady beauty he had fallen in love with. Raymond would be surprised and grateful to learn that Hattie was the one who had saved his daughter from Sam Tate. He would look into her eyes, say he forgave her for everything and ask if they could start over again. And, of course, Hattie's answer would be "yes."

But weeks, then months, passed and Hattie realized Raymond might not be coming after all. Hattie thought about it and realized it wouldn't be that surprising if Albertina had not told anyone about her humiliation. She might have told her mother, but Lullah would be just the kind of mother who would rather her daughter's disgrace remain hidden for the sake of her reputation, or even for the fear of losing Raymond to a murderous rampage, which would surely be his response if he knew. For all her disappointment, Hattie understood. She was well acquainted with the pain of loving and losing that man.

CHAPTER THIRTEEN

What little odd satisfaction Hattie got from trying to cause the ruin of her rival's daughter was diminished by her own troubles. She had been so caught up in the situation with Albertina, she had not noticed how many children were coming down with a sickness called Diphtheria. Her own Jerome had become ill and was getting sicker as the days went by. Three children that were close to Jerome's age had already died. This put fear into Hattie's heart. Jerome was the only tie she had to Raymond now, and she would not be able to live without a piece of him with her.

Hattie had been a very devoted Christian, but as Jerome's condition deteriorated, she worried that her prayers were not being answered. Hattie felt her faith beginning to falter. Was her son's sickness payback for what she had done?

Hattie knew she had to do something. She couldn't let Jerome die. A lot of the local families relied on home remedies they received from the local healer, a woman they called Tante Mona. Hattie had heard of this woman. She thought she must be a lot like Miz Sophie, the medicine woman she had often seen in Lowndes County, but Tante Mona had a much more evil reputation. People said she practiced voodoo, and Hattie had always been warned to stay away from that kind of magic and to trust in God instead. But God hadn't seen fit to bring Raymond back to her, and he hadn't answered her prayers to make little Jerome better.

Ignoring all the admonitions she'd ever heard against so-called black magic, Hattie furtively sought out the famous Tante Mona. The woman, who was the most mysterious person Hattie had ever met in her life, listened to her requests and came back with bags of dried roots to mix into a drink for Jerome. Then, she gave Hattie some more roots to mix into her own tea before bedtime. "Before you can find the love you seek, you must answer to those you've wronged," Tante Mona said mysteriously.

In the meantime, one of the young members that had just became a nurse's aide heard about Jerome's condition. She was able to get the doctor that she worked for to examine Jerome and give him a vaccine. The boy immediately began to improve, and though it took him awhile to return completely back to normal, Hattie knew her prayers had been answered. She didn't know whether it was the shot or Tante Mona's tea that was responsible, but she knew she had been willing to do anything to save her boy.

Hattie feared that whatever the old woman's potions had done for Jerome, they had failed to produce the desired personal effects on her own life. She was still alone – Raymond Peace had not returned to claim her – and lonelier than ever. There were times when she thought she would burn up for the sheer desire for a man's love and attention. That kind of lust was nothing but another torturous sin. And even worse, it was the beginning of a terrible nightmares that plunged her mind into the past. Hattie's nights were a torture of bad dreams about the people she'd hurt. Tante Mona's cure had turned out to be more of a curse, but Hattie couldn't tell anyone about that either.

Hattie spiraled into such a depression that even her fellow church members noticed. Most folks thought her ailment was just women's troubles. Folks gathered around her to pray for her and help her get through it. Hattie slowly regained her desire to change her life. She remembered Miz Sophie's chamomile tea had always helped her sleep in the past. She went back to that, abandoning Tante Mona's mysterious potions. There was no telling what was in that voodoo tea anyway. Hattie was determined to survive.

After the worst of Jerome's illness had passed, Hattie decided to move the family to Montgomery, Alabama. She had heard that there were great jobs there, and she felt the change of scenery would do her family good. The next fourteen years proved to be the blessing she had been seeking. Lewis went into business for himself, Carl decided on trade school, and brilliant Jerome was able to attend a black college there in Montgomery. He was so handsome and was always a hit with the ladies. However, when he met Susan Chalfont, he fell deeply in love and never turned back.

In the meantime, Hattie met a man named Charlie Gray. He was about her age, not too bad looking, and owned a gas station in the heart of the black community. When Hattie would walk by the store, Charlie Gray would always try to strike up a conversation. Hattie didn't mind exchanging pleasantries with the man, but for several months, she rebuffed his advances. She was still true in her heart to Raymond Peace though he was a dream she had given up long ago.

But Charlie Gray was persistent. Each day it seemed he added more and more talk to their simple exchanges. Soon, they were involved daily in full-blown conversations that lasted several minutes. Hattie found herself looking forward to speaking with Mr. Charlie Gray and was surprised to realize that she had started to dress herself and style her hair in ways that she thought he might find pleasing. He made no secret of the fact that he thought she was attractive. Hattie chuckled to herself as she stood before the mirror one day. She was wearing a dress that she knew he liked. She placed her new hat carefully on her head at just the right angle and admired her reflection. She wondered what he would say about it. It was a simple straw hat, like the ones she'd worn as a little girl. She had made the roses and other flowers that adorned it out of some old clothes, and she thought it looked gorgeous. Wearing the hat reminded her of Raymond Peace, because he used to say her hats and head wraps made her look royal, like a queen. Hattie felt like a queen as she stepped out into the sun and sauntered by Charlie Gray's gas station.

Charlie was standing out front and whistled when she walked by. Blushing, Hattie went up to him and they began a friendly exchange. To her surprise, Charlie asked her if she would go out to a nightclub with him and listen to some good blues music.

"Well, I don't know about that," Hattie said thoughtfully. She had found her way back to the Lord and was not too sure if she wanted to go to some den of sin to listen to what she thought of as the devil's music. She had heard that those clubs were nothing but trouble.

But Charlie was so convincing and charming that she agreed to go.

"I promise to protect you from any bad characters in the place. If there are any," Charlie said, grinning. "And I promise you'll like the music, Miss Hattie," he said. "They say you only hear with your ears what you have in your heart, and you don't look like you have no devil in your heart."

A goose walked over Hattie's grave at Charlie's words. If he only knew the things she had done. But Hattie had to believe there was something to it. Charlie believed there was nothing but good in her heart, so she tried to make it true. It was easy to forget the past in the company of Charlie Gray, who was a strong, cheerful man who loved the blues. They danced, had a good time, and Hattie had to confess that the music really was good. In fact, she thought it was great.

As the days, weeks, and months passed, their relationship became very strong. On their first year anniversary, Charlie decided to ask for Hattie's hand in marriage. Hattie was shocked. She had not expected to ever marry or even find love again. Her superstitious sisters and cousins warned her.

"Are you sure you want to get married again, Hattie? I don't know about that," Viola had said cautiously. The family had always thought the death of Lewis Durham was a sign of bad luck for Hattie. They were sure any new marriage she entered into might be doomed. But Hattie shook off the warnings. She told Charlie that she would marry him under one condition: that she be allowed to keep the last name "Durham." Not because she was holding on the memory of her late husband Lewis in any way, but because the last name tied her to her three sons. Everybody already knew her as Mrs. Durham, anyway. It would be awkward if she suddenly started calling herself something else.

Charlie raised his eyebrows in amusement and put up a hand to stop her protests. "Woman, I don't care if you call yourself the Queen of England, as long as you call yourself my wife," he declared, taking another pull on his big cigar. Hattie joined in his laughter. She and Mr. Charles Thomas Gray were married before family and friends a month later.

Charlie was so good to Hattie she hardly could believe her luck. He loved her so much, demonstrating the patience and affection that Hattie had craved all of her life. Under his caring attention, her memories of Raymond Peace started to fade just a little. Hattie thought less of her old lover and concentrated on life with her new husband.

But that new life was not to last for very long. Hattie had noticed that Charlie had a bad cough that seemed to get worse as the days went by. When Hattie would bring it to his attention, he would just say, "It's nothing, just them damn cigarettes, probably."

However, he continued to smoke. As Charlie's cough worsened and began producing blood, he finally decided to go to the doctor. The couple was given the bad news that Charlie had cancer and likely had less than six months to live. Hattie took the news harder than her husband. Charlie tried to comfort her, telling her that everything would be just fine. In his heart, however, he was resolved to his doom. He was just glad that Hattie had her boys to see her through. He made each of them promise to be strong and support their mother always.

Hattie stayed by Charlie's side, waiting on him hand and foot. However, four months and five days later Charlie died peacefully in their bed.

After his death, a worn out Hattie wondered just why God had taken her Charlie. Was it because of what she had done in the past? She felt sure she was being punished. Was it because she killed her first husband and Lullah Peace's baby? Not to mention what she had done to try to hurt Albertina Peace? Hattie was afraid she had lost her chance of ever finding and keeping a real love in her life. She was aware of the gossip swirling around her, saying that she was a spider who could not keep a husband alive.

Even worse, Hattie's nightmares returned with a vengeance. Sometimes she dreamed of a dead, crying baby. Sometimes the baby's face turned into that of Albertina Peace, still crying mournfully. Hattie felt hopelessness taking over. She stopped trying to hold on so tightly to her sanity, which seemed to slip away from her by the day.

Hattie woke up with a jolt. She had been dreaming again, dreaming about Charlie Gray and the short time they'd had together. Where was she now? She looked around in a fog, slowing recognizing where she was. Charlie Gray was a thing of the past.

"I'm so sorry," she whispered into the air. She believed she could be forgiven for Lewis, but not Raymond and Lullah's baby. She was sure that was why she had lost Charlie.

T hat morning the phone rang at Jerome and Susan Durham's house. Jerome stood before a mirror, tying his tie. Susan admired her husband's devastating good looks as she reached for the phone. In the past few years, his dark brown eyes had taken on an amber tone and the salt and pepper shades in his beard and moustache gave him a dignified and dashing appearance. He would make a fine official.

"The Durham residence," Susan answered the phone. She nodded and made a few comments as Jerome watched her from the mirror. She shook her golden brown hair back for his benefit, but then turned to speak with controlled horror into the phone.

"Oh, my goodness. No, one of us will be there right away," she said. "Yes, thank you. Goodbye."

She turned to Jerome who was waiting to hear what the fuss was about.

"Was that the hospital?" he said. "Is my mother all right?"

"I'm sure she's fine," Susan replied calmly. "She had a bad night. The nurse said she woke up screaming something about killing a baby."

"What?" Jerome said.

"I'm sure she just had a bad dream," Susan said reassuringly. "But who even knows anymore what your mother is talking about half the time? I'm just afraid it's going to get worse before it gets better. And we don't need any controversy from her right now when things are going so well."

"Is that your new code word for my mother's illness – controversy?" Jerome said. He was touchy lately on the subject of his mother. He and Susan talked often about what was to be done about Hattie, and he knew his wife was willing to consider more drastic measures than he was. Hattie had gotten to be more than a handful lately, and it was true she was less than respectful when it came to his wife Susan, whom Hattie had never liked. But she was still his mother. Jerome wanted to make sure that any solution they considered would be agreeable to her.

"Jerome, we both know how unpredictable she is, and a public hospital is not the place for her, not at a critical time like now. What if one of those nosy damn nurses goes to the press with one of your mother's delirious stories?" Jerome dismissed that.

"Old people go crazy all the time," he said. "I'm sure it's no reflection on me if my elderly mother says something out of hand every now and then."

Susan tried to control her frustration. Jerome could be so naïve sometimes.

"Maybe saying she didn't mean to kill a baby is 'out of hand,'" his wife said patiently. "But will people think it's simply out of hand if Hattie Durham implicates her son, who's seeking elected office, in the death of a prominent white doctor's only son?" That got his attention, Susan noted with satisfaction.

Jerome sat down nervously.

"What are we going to do, Susan?" Susan stood before the mirror in her pink satin slip. She smoothed her brown-gold hair, then went to stand behind Jerome, stroking his shoulders.

"Let me take care of this, honey," she said. "You concentrate on your campaign and let me deal with your mother. She needs to be someplace private, with someone who lives there who's paid to care for her, with the right medication and everything else she needs. And it needs to happen fast."

Jerome sighed. Susan waited. She knew how difficult it was for him, knew how guilty he felt at doing anything to betray his adoring mother. And that was exactly how Hattie would see it, but it had to be done. Jerome knew his wife was a competent, calculating woman. It was one of the things he loved most about her. She always went after what she wanted and emotions rarely got in her way. It made her a valuable partner to a politician.

In this case, as always, Susan's calculations were in his best interests. She was willing to handle all of their domestic affairs – from their children to his mother, who had become like one of their children – so that he could focus on his goals. In that way, she was very much like his mother, Jerome thought, though he would never dare say such a thing to either of them. Jerome Durham knew how much the women in his life loved him. He would do his best to deserve it.

So he agreed to Susan's terms, trusting that it would all turn out for the best. Susan would get the best care for Hattie despite the cold way his mother sometimes treated her. Susan was determined to keep Hattie safe from the world and keep everything she and her husband were building safe from Hattie.

"I'm going to the hospital," Susan said.

Jerome laughed as he stood up and took his wife by the waist. "Seeing you first thing after a bad dream is hardly going to calm her down," he said. "I'd better go."

"No, Jerome, you will not be late this morning. It's too important," Susan said. The neighborhood coalition that Jerome led was going to make a formal announcement declaring him their candidate of choice. Though he and Susan had been making the rounds for weeks, knocking on doors, speaking at churches and schools, the event they were holding this morning would formally kick off his campaign. "I'll handle Mother Durham. The nurse can give her something if she gets too upset if they haven't already. I know it's hard, but we've got to do what's best for her," Susan cajoled.

"Well, you hurry up, and join me as soon as you can," Jerome said. He examined the mirror one more time, thinking what a handsome couple he and his wife made. "I need you by my side."

He didn't have to worry, Susan thought, wondering how quickly she could be done at the hospital. She knew how important it was for her and Jerome to present a perfect picture to the public so that he could win the vote. She had been quietly putting plans in place to take care of her mother-in-law once and for all, though it had taken up until now to get Jerome to agree to let her handle things. Installing Mother Durham in a private place, with a private nurse who would follow instructions to the letter would be costly, but worth it. And the situation would hopefully only be short term, Susan thought, as she pulled on a pair of stylish leather gloves and checked her own appearance in the mirror. Hattie Durham was an old woman. She wouldn't live forever. And, if necessary, things could be hurried along with the right nurse and the right medications. Mother Durham wouldn't be a problem for much longer. Susan kissed her husband and hurried out the door.

CHAPTER FIFTEEN

As Susan drove to check on her mother-in-law, she continued to think about the secrets in her life that she had and how she had shared them with her husband. She knew that her husband had shared many secrets with his mother. If only the old woman would just die, all their troubles would be over.

She quickly parked her car in front of the building in a reserved space. She wasn't worried since everyone knew her car, and she felt that she could do what she wanted.

When she reached the ward, she looked around for the nurse who had called their home that morning, Nurse Joyce. She was one of the few nurses at the hospital whom Susan trusted, not because she was particularly more competent than the others, but because she seemed more professional. Unlike the other nurses there, Joyce was not taken in by Hattie's situation or her little stories. Susan thought Joyce might make a perfect private nurse for her mother in law for the right price.

Now, she had to handle Hattie. Susan smoothed her hair and took a deep breath before entering the room. Her mother-in-law was sitting up in bed.

"Hello, Mother Durham," Susan said, bounding in with a smile. Hattie scowled, but Susan didn't let it stop her from leaning over to kiss the air near the old woman's cheek.

"I've got great news for you this morning," Susan said. Hattie ignored the comment.

"Where's Jerome?" she demanded.

"Oh, Mother Durham," Susan sighed, choosing to ignore Hattie's question. "The doctor says you are doing really well, and we can take you out of here soon. Isn't that exciting news?"

"Why are you all trying to get rid of me?" Hattie demanded. "First, you bring me here, and now that I'm settled in just fine, starting to like this place, now you want to take me someplace else."

"Because, old woman, you started losing your mind long ago, but it's already so gone you don't even realize it," Susan snapped. It had been a tiring morning already at the hospital, and her nerves were frayed. First, the nurse she had spoken to on the phone had run to her with more stories of Hattie's behavior. Then, Susan had run into Jerome's brother, Carl, as he was leaving his mother's room. He was moving slow and wore a stunned look on his face as he left his mother's room. Seeing the state he was in, Susan had spoken with him briefly. Now, she confronted her mother-in-law with all the trouble she had caused. "You have blabbed all kinds of private family business to these nurses."

"Why would I do that?" Hattie mumbled irritably.

"Oh, Lord, you don't even remember," Susan groaned. "That, Mother Durham, is the reason why we have to get you away from here to someplace more private, so you don't mess around and say something to mess things up for all of us. Think of Jerome."

"Jerome," Hattie said, sitting up straighter. "Where is he, anyway? Why doesn't he come see me no more?

Carl and Junior ain't even been here to see me once," she grumbled. "You're the one keeping them away, ain't you? You think you got to control everything."

"No, Mother Durham, but I've got to control you or else you will destroy us with that dirty blabbermouth of yours," Susan spat. "Talking about committing adultery, killing babies, and God knows what else you've said around here. And, to prove my point, Carl was just here, but you clearly don't even remember," Susan went on. "He told me you thought he was his dead daddy, Lewis."

Hattie frowned, trying to remember. She thought she'd had a dream in which she was talking to Lewis. He looked good as though he had never taken a beating at all, but Hattie thought maybe that was God's grace. She had tried to explain to him the reasons for her actions, telling him she did it for her sons.

"You was too hurt to live and too weak to die, and I had our boys to look after," she had told him. "I hope it brought you a little peace, too, Lewis."

He said he forgave her and seemed to fade away in tears. Now, Hattie gasped in horror. Had she unburdened herself to her son, thinking all the while that she was dreaming about talking to his father? Junior was Lewis' namesake but his younger brother Carl was the one who looked the most like their daddy. Hattie felt her daughter-in-law was watching her intently and Hattie realized that she knew.

"Is Carl all right?" Hattie said.

"Don't worry, Mother Durham, he's not going to say anything," Susan said, ignoring Hattie's question. "He didn't even tell his brothers, just me. Carl won't do anything to hurt your name or his brother's chances in this election," she went on.

"Some of us would like to protect the family's reputation, even if you don't mind who knows all of the terrible things you've done."

Susan folded her arms stubbornly. Her words seemed to have given Hattie pause. The old woman looked up slowly.

"Yes, child, I have done some terrible things in my time," she said. "I have committed some horrible sins. But every bad thing I ever done was because of the love caught up in it." She looked at Susan. "Even what I did for you."

"Lord, I let those white people think I was crazy," Hattie continued, shaking her head with the memory. "Walking up there on the water tower at night. I told all those folks my man left me, and I didn't want to live no more." Hattie had found the charade easy to play. All she had to do was recall how it had felt to lose Raymond, and her broken heart showed. Standing over Chancelly Foster's body, she had somehow made them believe her story, that she had gone up on the tower intending to throw herself over the edge, that Chancelly had seen her, tried to stop her, and had fallen himself in the attempt.

But that story wasn't the truth at all. Hattie hadn't told anyone else who else she had seen up there that night, who else she'd talked to, or who else Chancelly had seen or talked to, for that matter. Had they checked his body for prints, there would have been no evidence that he'd ever been near Hattie Durham, had never grabbed her arms or shoulders in an attempt to keep her from jumping.

"Those people hated me so bad that night," Hattie said. "There I was, crazy but alive, and there he was, a young, rich white boy with all of the future ahead of him dead on the ground because he wanted to save my life. At least that's what I let them think."

"It was a sin for me to lie like that and keep it up all these years, but I did it for you," she stood up slowly and looked her daughter-in-law in the eye. Susan refused to be intimidated.

"You didn't do that for me," she said. "You told that lie for your precious Jerome."

Yes, Hattie thought, her precious son Jerome. Raymond's son. She would do anything to keep him happy, and that's why she'd spent all these years helping him protect his wife. She had made a promise to do for the son what she could not do for the father. She had thought that just maybe protecting this one of Raymond's sons was a way to make up for the loss of the unborn one.

"Like I said, everything bad I ever done was because of me loving somebody," Hattie countered. "Have you ever done anything for love? You sure didn't kill that boy because you loved Jerome. You pushed him over the side to keep people from knowing what you were doing up there with him."

Susan's eyes narrowed with anger. How dare this old woman presume to know what had happened with Chancelly Foster, who was no hero no matter what people had been told.

Susan hissed, caught up in her own memories now. She had been new to Alabama, an attractive Creole girl toying with a chance to pass. Chancelly had been taken with her, intimated at marriage, then rejected her. Despite her blond looks, Susan Chalfont wasn't the white girl she appeared to be.

Never one to take insults lightly, Susan had taken an opportunity when she saw it, and, in the end, Chancelly had simply paid the price. Jerome Durham had been her savior. He was a handsome young man with a bright future, and he adored her. Susan thought it wasn't a bad outcome, all things considered. Not knowing exactly what had transpired between her and Chancelly, Jerome had assured her that he would take care of her, and he had. He had enlisted his mother's help, and the rest was history. Susan shook her head as if to shake off the bad memories. In the meantime, Hattie had started to rock and moan.

"I lied for you because Jerome asked me to save you. He wanted you so bad. I don't know why, but he said he had to have you, and he asked me to help you, so I did. I let people think that boy's fall was my fault and kept you from a murder charge so that my Jerome could have a chance at what you already gave Chancelly Foster for free!"

Infuriated, Susan slapped her mother-in-law as hard as she could. Hattie's head rocked back from the impact, and her feet slipped out from under her, shooting forward as she fell backward.

"Mother Durham!" Susan called out, too late, as the old woman fell. Hard. Her head hit the floor with a dull, but resounding thump. Susan saw Nurse Lisa rush in from behind her and kneel at the old woman's side. Susan had no idea how long the nurse had been standing there. It didn't matter.

"Nurse, what happened here was an accident," she

said pointedly. Lisa had rung for assistance and was checking the old woman's pulse. "Anything else would present a terrible inconvenience to my husband's campaign." Susan waited. Hattie Durham stayed silent, and the silence was blessed.

CHAPTER SIXTEEN

I t was remarkable, but Hattie was still alive. Lisa didn't say a word to Susan, but brushed past her, all but pushing her out of the way as the emergency team she had called rushed Hattie to have emergency tests done. Susan stood in disbelief as they quickly took Hattie for a CAT scan. Never one to be accused of inaction, Susan called Jerome then waited nervously for her husband to come to the hospital. She was so nervous that she actually began biting her perfectly manicured nails. She stopped when she realized the damage she had done. She made a note to make an appointment as soon as possible. In the meantime, she would have to remember to hide her hands from the family, who would surely notice her ragged nails. They all knew Susan well enough to know the pride she took in looking polished and never having a hair out of place. Her sisters-in-law especially would notice and remark on how her hands looked, probably behind her back. Susan clasped her hands together and waited for Jerome to arrive.

When Jerome got there, he rushed in with both his brothers and their wives in tow. Just then, the doctor came out and told the family that Hattie had sustained a serious head injury in her fall. There was bleeding in her brain. They could operate to stop the hemorrhage, but she would likely never be able to breathe on her own. Or the family could decide not to take measures to keep the elderly Mrs. Durham alive. Without the surgery, the internal bleeding would eventually kill her, likely sooner than later.

The family went somberly to the waiting room to pray and discuss their difficult decision. Susan performed perfectly as the councilman's supportive wife, holding onto Jerome as they entered the room. Her composed exterior concealed her frustration. She had thought this was all over with Hattie's fall, but the stubborn old woman had hung on.

Speaking carefully, Susan was the first to break the silence. "If I was Mother Durham, I would want for you all to let me go."

The eldest brother, Junior, replied, "We will remember that if this happens to you."

Susan's expression showed her displeasure with his sarcastic comment, but now was not the time to argue with her husband's brother. She told herself that the man was just upset, though she would probably put him in check later. Junior's wife, Donetta, noticed the sour look on Susan's pale face and intervened.

"I think Susan is just trying to get you all to think this all the way through," Donetta said. Susan was surprised at the support. She and Donetta had never gotten along particularly well, but now Susan made a mental note to make more of an effort at a relationship with her sister-in-law. Donetta walked over to Junior and put her arms around him, soothing him.

Junior was thinking about his last visit with Hattie, a couple of days ago. She had noticed him looking at the nurse and told him to stop.

"Boy, you always were too mannish for your

own good, but I guess Donetta knew what she was getting when she married you," Hattie had chuckled. "Y'all thought we didn't know that girl was pregnant, but that's why we rushed the wedding ceremony to keep you all out of shame." Lewis, Jr. was too cocky to be embarrassed but he didn't appreciate his mother insinuating that he would ever be unfaithful to his current wife, Donetta. Already twice around the marriage block, Junior felt sure that Donetta, who liked to wear bright-colored wigs and could shoot pool as well as he, was his true soul mate.

"Mama, you know she don't mind if I look as long as I don't touch," he had grinned.

Now, Junior smiled at the memory. Over time, his mother had come to embrace his clever, friendly wife. If only Hattie could see Donetta now, standing up for Susan. She would probably choke in disbelief. He knew Hattie couldn't stand Susan.

"What will Ma'dear think about being tied up to an oxygen tank all the time?" Donetta was saying.

At that, Carl stood up and abruptly left the room. His wife, Trudy, looked around at his brothers' faces. Jerome looked bewildered and even scared. Junior just looked mad. Trudy rushed out of the room after her husband. After a moment, Susan followed them.

Trudy found Carl in the hallway, looking out a window. The distraught man was thinking about his last conversation with his mother when she had mistaken him for the father he resembled so much. His dead father. What was it she had said to him thinking he was the late Lewis Durham?

"Too hurt to live and too weak to die." He whispered

the phrase to himself, thinking how perfectly the words described Hattie's own condition right now. That was what she had used to judge her decision on what to do when their father was in that state. Would she want her sons to handle her life based on that criteria?

"Carl, honey, are you all right?" Trudy said, coming up behind him. He turned to speak to her, but stopped when he saw Susan was also standing there.

"I'm fine, baby, I just needed some fresh air," he told his wife. His gaze was still locked on his sister-in-law.

"Your brothers need you in there," Trudy said. "You all need to make a decision so the doctors can tend to your mother."

"Trudy, I need to talk to Carl for a moment," Susan interrupted. Trudy turned to look at Susan questioningly. She had no idea what the woman wanted with Carl. She should be with her own husband right now. Trudy clung to Carl's arm, but he shook her off.

"Trudy, why don't you go get us some coffee?" he said absently. He was still looking at Susan, which vexed Trudy.

"Y'all hurry up, then," she said, trying to conceal her irritation. An argument was the last thing the family needed right now. Throwing a last glance at Susan, Trudy rushed off to get the coffee. Susan approached Carl slowly.

"Carl, I know you're thinking about what Hattie said to you," she began.

"Yes, right now I'm thinking about what the hell she did to my father," he fumed. "What gave her the right to make that choice? And now me, Junior, and Jerome have to make the same kind of choice about her."

Frustrated, he turned to face the window again. Susan touched him gently on the elbow.

"It's not the same thing," she said.

"Yes, it is," Carl said. "Right now we are being asked to choose whether my mother should live or die, aren't we?"

"Yes, but it still is not the same thing," Susan said. "Carl, what your mother did was unthinkable, I know, but you have to put yourself in her shoes." She couldn't believe she was sticking up for Hattie, but she was.

"You know that your mother wouldn't have ever done anything like that if she thought it wasn't the best thing for you and your brothers. Why would she have thought that being without a father was better for the family? Think about it, Carl." Pulling on his arm, she turned the big man around to face her. Carl's face was crumpled with emotion.

"He did used to hit her sometimes," he said, his voice cracking. "Sometimes he'd hit me and Junior too. He'd whip our asses good if we got out of line, and sometimes it seemed like he did it for nothing." Carl nodded slowly, reminiscing. "Only Jerome missed out on that action."

Susan nodded too, thinking it made sense that Hattie would try to eliminate anyone who possibly posed a threat to Jerome. It was why she had been willing to take the blame in Chancelly Foster's death and probably the reason for a million other things the woman had done in her lifetime. Protecting Jerome and making sure he had everything in the world he wanted seemed to have been Hattie Durham's main priority.

"Well, Hattie loved you all, and she did what she felt she had to do to make sure you were safe and happy,"

Susan said softly. "So please don't tell Jerome and Junior about it. Please let them make up their minds what to do without any anger or confusion over how your father died. Let them have some peace of mind," she persuaded.

Carl looked at her with stormy eyes. After a moment, he relented. "I'm not going to say anything to my brothers about what she did. I'm never going to say a word about it because it would kill them," he said.

"But I know you're not doing this because you care that much about my mother," he added. "You and her never did get along that well."

Susan looked back at him calmly. "It doesn't mean I want her to die, Carl," she said. "After all, Jerome's my husband, and I know what this is doing to him. I'm just trying to make things as easy as possible for him, given the circumstances."

"And just what are the circumstances, anyway, Sue?" Carl said. Susan winced. She hated it when people shortened her name. "You were alone with my mother when she fell, weren't you? She had no business even being out of bed."

Just then Trudy rushed up to them, bearing a tray full of coffee cups, cream, and sugar.

"Let's take this into the family and see how everyone is," Trudy said, cutting their conversation short. Susan smiled grimly and followed her brother and sister-in-law back into the room.

"Are you all right, bro?" Junior asked Carl as they reentered the waiting room. Jerome slapped Carl on the back, drawing him into the circle. They talked quietly as Trudy distributed coffee and condiments. The three women sat back silently as the brothers agreed that they should go ahead with the surgery. They wanted to save their mother.

"I'm sure Ma'dear would not want us making a decision to end her life," Jerome reasoned. "That's a decision only God should make," Jerome reasoned. He knew his wife would understand his choice.

"Of course, Jerome," Susan said, giving in sweetly. "I hope I didn't offend anyone with my suggestion earlier. I was just thinking of Mother Durham's comfort."

Jerome embraced his wife, then kissed her. He was grateful to have a wife as beautiful, caring, and strong as Susan. He simply didn't know what he would do without her.

"Well, you're right that it's God's decision and His alone," Carl said. He was resolved. "We'll let the doctors do what they do best, and put mama's life in His hands, not ours."

After a long wait, the Durham family was glad to hear that the surgery had been successful. The doctors were able to stop the bleeding in Hattie's brain. But, as they had warned, she remained unconscious. Still, every day it seemed that she was doing a little better, though she still could not breathe on her own.

After a couple of weeks, Jerome informed his wife that he wanted to bring his mother home to live with them. At first, Susan was prepared to object. She didn't want to put up with Hattie any more even if the old lady was unconscious. But she knew Jerome felt so guilty over what had happened to Hattie, that he was not going to change his mind. She took charge and started making the necessary arrangements.

Usually hospitals would not allow life support to be

set up at a private residence, but the Durhams were in a position to get the director to do what they wanted; they were able to bring Hattie home. She received around-the-clock care from a team of shift nurses.

As the days went by, Susan saw how obsessively Jerome was monitoring Hattie's care. In her opinion, he was spending too much time watching over his mother. He was losing sleep worrying, and his campaign had started to suffer. That was unacceptable after all they had worked for. Hattie needed to be gone so that Jerome could focus and move on. Susan decided to take things into her own hands.

Once she made her decision, Susan acted quickly. She called the nurse that was due to arrive that morning for the day shift and told her not to come in, because there had been a schedule mix-up and they were double-booked. It was a bold lie.

Then, Susan asked the current nurse on duty if she could stay just a few minutes longer. Susan wanted Jerome to leave for to work before the nurse left. Jerome lingered that morning, suddenly reluctant to leave his home. He kept looking in on Hattie.

Susan suppressed her frustration, drawing him back into the kitchen and kissing him reassuringly. She promised him a good dinner and a sexy evening, but urged him to hurry up and get to work. Finally, he left, and she told the nurse that she could leave. At first, the woman resisted, stating that her orders were that Hattie had to have a nurse present at all times.

"It's all right. Your replacement assures me that she's just a short ways away," Susan lied again smoothly. "And I'll be here with her." When the nurse hesitated, Susan's tone became firm. "It's all right. You can leave now."

Gathering her things with a huff, the stocky little nurse finally left the house. Susan watched her walk away but waited a few minutes to make sure she was completely alone with her mother-in-law. Without further delay, she got up and unplugged the machine, then left the room. Hattie struggled for breath. Susan continued to check on Hattie every thirty minutes, hoping that the troublesome old woman had breathed her last, disappointed each time to find her still alive. Her long, raspy breaths grated on Susan's nerves. Jerome was due home in two hours, and Susan was getting angrier by the minute. She had expected Hattie to be dead long before he got home.

She went to check on her mother-in-law one last time, wearily planning to resort to plan B. But when she went in, the room was still and silent. Susan stood still, listening to be sure. Hattie had finally taken her last breath. Susan plugged the machine back in and called her husband, crying.

❧ Epilogue ❧

The congregation had already started to gather for the funeral. An old man slipped into an aisle seat in a row near the back of the church. He tried not to attract attention, but his impressive height and distinctive features drew many eyes. A woman seated a few rows ahead of him glanced at him, did a double take, looked again, then tapped her husband on the shoulder.

"He looks just like Councilman Durham, doesn't he?" she whispered.

"Ssshh!" her husband whispered back.

Raymond Peace had come to pay his respects to the woman he had once loved. He had moved his family out of the state after his wife's miscarriage, but came back occasionally on trips to his father-in-law's first lumber yard. He was on such a trip when he learned that Hattie had passed.

Over the years he had tried to put her out of his mind, refusing to deal with the conflicting emotions that memories of her could bring. What could make a woman plan to carry out another woman's murder? And how could he have loved such a person himself? Raymond knew he would never be able to understand Hattie, but he sure hoped she had found some measure of peace.

The processional was starting, and the family was making its way down the aisle. Raymond did a double take of his own as Hattie's three adult sons walked down with their families. One of the men was a mirror image of Raymond himself, only 30 years younger with a distinguished air about him, and wavy salt and pepper hair that was still mostly black. Raymond had thought he would sit through the service in somber reflection, but tears were running freely down his face and the funeral had only just begun.

"We are here today to celebrate the homegoing of one of our most beloved members, Mrs. Hattie Eloise Durham. The family asks that we concentrate not on the difficulties of their mother's last days, but on the spectrum of her whole life – which included a wealth of family and friends – and of the love she held in her charitable heart for each and every one of us," the Reverend Bradley Donald Cooper intoned.

"There was something Mother Durham always used to say, and it's something that she would want all of us to remember as we go out into the world," he continued. "Sister Hattie liked to say that every child deserves to be loved. Did you hear that, church?" The congregation responded with shouts and handclaps.

Hattie's cousin, Doe, burst into tears. She knew Hattie's favorite saying had been born from her own experiences as a child who thought her own family had not loved her. Hattie had been like a sister to her ever since coming to live with their family scores of years ago. The little girl had been forever scarred by being sent away without an explanation. Jerome put his arm around his aunt's shaking shoulders.

"Every child deserves to be loved!" the reverend repeated. "That's right. No matter who the mother is, no matter who the father is. No matter if they're black, white, red, or brown. No matter if they're dark or light, rich or poor, healthy or afflicted. Every child deserves to be loved."

A young girl who had once confided in Hattie sniffled loudly then began to sob. The old woman's kindness to her had helped turn her life around. Susan Durham tightened her lips as others began to express their grief. It was bound to be an emotional ceremony, but she hoped things would stay dignified.

"So now, with those words from your very own lips," the reverend continued, "You can rest assured, Mother Durham, you who were once a little child yourself and still are but an innocent child in the eyes of the Lord, that you, too, deserved love. And you had so much of it here in the hearts of your three sons and their beautiful families. You were not only a mother to them but to all of us in this church family."

So far, the three Durham men had been stoic, but now, Carl, the middle one, broke down in grief. Of the three, he seemed to be taking his mother's death the hardest. His wife, Trudy, nodded her approval as Lewis, the oldest brother, put his arm around his brother's shoulder, and Jerome reached back to clasp his arm. Trudy thought Carl had been acting strange ever since his last visit with Hattie, the day before she died. It was as if he had already been struck by grief prior to her death, so it was good to see the family rally around him like this. Trudy even stood aside tolerantly as their phony sister-in-law Susan turned around and embraced Carl.

As she withdrew from Carl, Susan took the opportunity to see who else was there. She spotted a group of nurses from the hospital, huddled together in one the pews. They would be all over Jerome at the reception, she thought and pressed her lips together even tighter. She certainly hoped they were all registered to vote. Susan locked gazes with Lisa for a moment, then she looked away. The reverend's deep voice continued to ring out.

"God rest your soul, our beautiful Mother Durham. We will all miss your wise counsel and your loving touch, but we will never forget you. We will always love you. And we know that you will get your reward in Heaven. Amen."

Jerome Durham reached for his wife's pale, slim hand. He wore on his hand the thick, gold embossed ring that the council had given him to proclaim him their candidate for the next election. Susan Durham looked straight ahead and smiled.

❧ THE END ☙

CPSIA information can be obtained
at www.ICGtesting.com
Printed in the USA
LVOW13s1006191117
556805LV00020B/1206/P